Going Rogue

GOING ROGUE
(at Hebrew School)

CASEY BRETON

Green
Bean
Books

Green Bean Books

First published in 2020 by Green Bean Books,
c/o Pen & Sword Books Ltd,
47 Church Street, Barnsley, S. Yorkshire, S70 2AS
www.greenbeanbooks.com

ISBN 978-1-78438-539-2
PJ Library ISBN 978-1-78438-543-9

Library of Congress Cataloging-in Publication Data available

Typeset in Garamond 12/16
by JCS Publishing Services Ltd, www.jcs-publishing.co.uk
Printed and bound by CPI Group (UK) Ltd, Croydon, CR0 4YY

Everyone goes to synagogue for a different reason.
Garfinkle goes to synagogue to speak with God.
I go to synagogue to speak with Garfinkle.

Harry Golden

•

Shlemiel vs. *Shlimazel* (Yiddish)
A *shlemiel* is somebody who often spills his soup.
A *shlimazel* is the person it lands on.

CHAPTER
1

There are three things I'm really into. Been into them all my life, and probably always will. I'm like a loyal dog that way.

Number One: Star Wars. Believe me when I say that I'm a walking, talking Star Wars encyclopedia. I've seen every Star Wars movie 400 times. Okay, so maybe not 400 exactly. But pretty close. I've also read every book related to Star Wars. Plus, I've written my own. It's called *My Life as an Ewok: A True Story*. I'm also working on a script for the next Star Wars episode which, as it turns out, is not as easy as it sounds. I've been hammering away at it for the past three weeks and it's still not finished. I have a little Yoda figurine who sits on my desk when I write, and whenever I get stuck I look at him.

He just kind of sits there and looks back at me.

We look at each other, in silence.

Sometimes, more words come to me and I keep writing.

But mostly I just get hungry, call it a day, and get a snack.

People ask me what I love most about Star Wars. And my answer is: Everything. Obviously. I mean, what is there not to love? It has insane amounts of action *in space*, amazing special effects, and the weirdest, best creatures in the entire known universe. And, good versus evil. Can't forget about that. You got your good guys and your bad guys and there they are duking it out *in space*. You never have to scratch your head wondering who to root for in Star Wars. It's the good guys. It's like having an ultimate favorite galactic team that you always want to win, and their arch-nemesis team that you always want defeated. Can't get any better than that.

Number Two: Science. There's a very good chance that when I grow up, I'll be a scientist. That's because I want to know the answers to *everything*.

I haven't decided which area of science I'll end up in, though.

I could see getting into robotics. Robots are crazy cool. Or maybe chemistry. I built a science lab in my basement where I do experiments, like making things explode and mixing random liquids to make terrible-smelling potions.

My best so far is Potion #17: mouthwash, hot sauce, and the liquid from a can of tuna fish. Even our scrappy dog, Champ, had to leave the room when I brewed that one, and she likes to eat trash for fun.

But most likely I'll be an astrophysicist. Because, really, is there anything more awesome than the universe?

Number Three: Good ol' American football. Can't get enough of it. During football season, I watch every game I possibly can from one of my two designated spots—far left side of the couch if my team, the Patriots, are not playing; far right if they are. You know, so that everything goes *right* for them. There are no exceptions to this rule. If for some strange reason the right side of the couch spontaneously combusted and the Patriots were just about to play, I'd sit on top of the smoldering couch ashes on the right side and watch the game.

I keep a notebook and a pencil in my backpack and draw out football plays every day during lunch. At six plays per lunch period, five days a week, and forty weeks in the school year, times two years (been doing it since third grade), that's roughly 2,400 plays—and a lot of notebooks. I figure this will come in handy in case I want to have a side career as a coach for the National Football League. Not that I haven't considered being a player. It's just that I'm scrawny, which is great for darting in between players and being fast on the field during recess, but kind of risky when you get to the professional level. I know a lot about concussions.

This is because my parents lecture me about concussions every time I bring up the subject of me playing in the East Bay Football League, which happens to be one of my number one dreams.

I know all about the East Bay Football League. This is because there are a bunch of kids at school in the league and I'm an ace eavesdropper. I secretly listen in when they're talking about their games and coaches and players and what drills they run during practice and, well, I'd be lying if I said I wasn't crazy jealous. Also, I'm not blind. I see them all wearing their EBFL jerseys, which basically look exactly like real NFL jerseys. The kind I don't have because they cost beaucoup bucks. Also, I pass by the EBFL games and practices four times every week. Which feels like torture.

"Why can't you just stick to flag football?" my parents ask. "It's so much safer." They say this because they don't understand.

Don't get me wrong. I like flag football. I like it a lot. But when you get to be my age, and you've been playing flag football for as long as I have, you start to crave something a little more. Like wearing a real uniform, with a real helmet, and actually tackling real players instead of just grabbing the flags out of their belt.

"Are you saying the players in flag football aren't real?" Mom asks. I find this question extremely annoying, because she knows the answer.

"And all this time I was sure they were real," Dad says sarcastically.

"Everyone knows they're not," I reply, just to throw them for a loop. "They're holograms."

"Point for Avery," Dad says, and draws an imaginary tally mark in the air.

"Must you encourage his snarkiness?" Mom snaps at him. Then she turns to me. "And the answer is no. Besides, you wouldn't be able to play anyway," she reminds me. "You have Hebrew school on Tuesdays and Sundays."

Which brings me to the one thing I am really, really *not* into. Hebrew school. I've been going ever since kindergarten. It wasn't so bad back then. Probably because back then I didn't know any better. But now I do. And it's starting back up next week after one whole, perfect, entire summer without it.

The reason Hebrew school is at the top of my "anti" list is because, the way I see it, Hebrew school is a dream-crusher that goes totally against all the things I'm really into.

Case in point: Nothing about Hebrew school has anything—anything!—to do with Star Wars. In fact, last year I invented a little game for myself to confirm this unfortunate fact by answering Hebrew school questions with Star Wars references, and noting my teacher's response.

> HST (Hebrew School Teacher): Who remembers King Ahasuerus's evil aide from the story of Purim?
>
> Me: Darth Maul.
>
> HST: *(Takes a long inhale through her nose and a long exhale through her mouth. I think it's her way of not killing me. It seems to work.)* Not quite. Anyone else?
>
> Me, again: Haman.
>
> HST: *(Sighs with relief.)* Thank you, Avery. Yes. Haman.
>
> Me: But it might as well have been Darth Maul.

5

I mean, really, what's the difference between the two? Both served as the right-hand man to a crummy emperor, both wielded incredible power, both used that power to master evil, and both tortured anyone who didn't agree with their beliefs.

HST: Interesting point, but …

Me: And both had gnarly mangled faces behind their creepy masks and used red lightsabers.

HST: (*Blank stare.*)

See what I mean? Star Wars and Hebrew school. It's like mouth wash, hot sauce, and tuna fish liquid. People seem to find the mixture offensive.

Same thing with science and Hebrew school.

Here's the thing: Grown-ups are always telling kids how important school is, how we need to pay attention and work hard in school. Okay. Fine. I get it. I pay attention. I work hard. I don't *love* school, but it's better than being a moisture farmer on Tatooine, like Luke Skywalker was when he was my age.

My favorite subject in school is, obviously, science. (I've been told recess is not a subject, and in PE we're learning ballroom dance which all the mothers think is fabulous but which I argue is not a sport, and therefore PE is no longer my other favorite subject.) Although my science teacher won't let us explode things ("not appropriate," she tells me), we *have* learned some pretty amazing stuff in science.

The Big Bang. One word: Whoa.

Dinosaurs. Bring it. Especially the dilophosaurus, which would make an excellent Star Wars creature.

Evolution. Example: My parents say I eat like a Neanderthal. I say better than a Homo heidelbergensis.

All good stuff, right?

But then I go to Hebrew school and it's like I'm in some weird parallel universe where none of the things I'm really into even exist.

My HST tells us that God created the universe in six days.

"What about the Big Bang?" I ask.

She smiles a little nervously and says, "Well, that's also true."

"Also true?" I ask. "How?"

She closes her eyes and rubs her forehead like she suddenly got a headache. "Honey, that's a conversation for another time, okay?"

That "another time" hasn't come yet.

"Were there dinosaurs on Noah's Ark?"

"Ummm." She scrunches up her nose and taps her chin. "I don't believe so," she says.

"Did Adam and Eve also evolve from early primates?" I ask.

"Ooh, interesting question. But how about we put that one on the back burner for now?"

I'm afraid everything on the back burner is going to burn.

And, to make it all worse, not only do I have to go to *extra* school twice a week to learn things that go totally against what I'm into, I'll never be able to convince my parents to let me play in the East Bay Football League because practice is on Tuesdays at 4:00 and games are played on Sunday mornings—the exact and precise days and times of Hebrew school.

Coincidence?

I think not.

I believe my Hebrew school teachers have devised a master plan to ruin my life.

Over the years, I've tried just about everything to get out of Hebrew school.

Pretending to be sick.

Sneaking out the back door of the synagogue and hiding in the creepy alley. The mangy mice and I had a pretty intense stare down. Eventually, they won and I had to sneak back in.

I even signed up to be in the spelling club at my regular school just because their meetings conflicted perfectly with Hebrew school. But my parents didn't fall for it. "Aren't you the kid who argued that learning how to spell has been a waste of time ever since the invention of spell check on computers?" they reminded me.

"Why do I even have to go to Hebrew school?"

I've only asked this question about a million times.

And they've given me about a million answers. Only problem is, none of their answers add up. Here is a sample of their attempts:

"I had to go to Hebrew school. You have to go to Hebrew school. It's tradition."

To which I reply, "Did you know that rabbis used to swing chickens over their heads on Yom Kippur to erase their sins, and that some still do? That's also a tradition."

After a long moment of silence, my mom says, "No, I didn't know that."

"How do you know which traditions to keep, then? Do you think we should still whip chickens around our heads, for tradition's sake?"

"Nice try, Avery. But you're still going to Hebrew school."

They give me speeches about famous Jewish people, like Albert Einstein and Sandy Koufax. "Hebrew school will teach you to be proud to be Jewish," Mom says.

Dad says, "Hebrew school will give you a chance to make friends with other Jewish kids."

"What difference does it make if my friends are Jewish or not?" I remind him that it's not nice to choose friends based on how they look, or their religion, or anything other than who they are inside and how they treat others.

He kisses my forehead and calls me a *mensch*. "Maybe you'll learn what the word *mensch* means in Hebrew school," he laughs.

"First of all, *mensch* is Yiddish, Dad, not Hebrew. And second of all, I already know that *mensch* means *a good kid* because Bubs taught me." Bubs is short for *bubbe*, which means grandma in Yiddish.

He suggests that maybe Bubs should be a teacher at my

Hebrew school, which I think is not a half-bad idea. At least she appreciates Star Wars.

I like Bubs a lot. She teaches me the secrets of making the world's best chicken soup and funny words in Yiddish that she learned from *her* grandmother. Words like *plotz*, which is my favorite. I teach her all the best plays in football. So with the new Hebrew school year looming on the horizon—just thinking about it makes me want to *plotz!*—I ask her the question without an answer.

"Bubs, why do Mom and Dad make me go to Hebrew school?"

"You're a smart boy to ask such a good question," she says. A very promising start, I think. She puts her arm around me and gives me a warm squeeze. "The answer is simple."

Yes, finally! A good, simple answer from a reliable source.

"Because you're the next generation in a long chain. A link between the past and the future."

I'll admit, it sounds cool. Like something Yoda might say. But honestly, it really doesn't make that much sense. I think Bubs can see that I don't totally get what she means.

She pats my hand and says, "Don't worry, *bubeleh*. When you're my age, you'll understand."

The problem is that I'm sixty-four years away from being her age. And by the time I get to her age, she won't even be that age anymore. Plus, I'll be done with Hebrew school—if it hasn't killed me—so I don't see how this is helpful to me right now.

I explain to Mom and Dad that I've already wasted 400

days of my life sitting inside that stuffy old synagogue learning nothing.

They say education is never a waste. They tell me not to be so dramatic. They tell me to look on the bright side.

"What bright side?"

"After your bar mitzvah, you'll never have to go to Hebrew school again."

If that's the bright side, I'm afraid to know what the dark side looks like.

First of all, my bar mitzvah is not for another three years. *That's three more years of my life.* That's practically as long as it takes a space probe to reach Saturn.

I think I'd rather give that a try.

Second of all, a bar mitzvah sounds like torture. Here's what a bar mitzvah is: Some poor kid has to get dressed up in fancy clothes and stand in front of the whole congregation with everyone staring at him while he chants a bunch of prayers in Hebrew and gives a speech about everything he learned about being Jewish in wonderful Hebrew school.

I hate wearing fancy clothes.

I hate people staring at me.

I don't like chanting prayers, especially in a language I barely understand.

The only speeches I like giving are on the subjects of Star Wars, science, and football.

I'm pretty sure I haven't learned anything about being Jewish.

I don't think Hebrew school is wonderful. Saying it would make me a liar.

And every time I lie my face turns bright red. Which is super-embarrassing.

My parents remind me about the party afterwards. "Doesn't that part sound fun?" they ask.

"Not more fun than playing in the East Bay Football League," I explain. "Which I'll never be able to do because of Hebrew school." I look at them for a long time, then add, "You know what it's like to have a dream crushed?"

"Oh, honestly, Avery," Mom says in her very frustrated voice. She walks away.

"Bring out the violins," Dad says. He walks away.

Here's the thing. Grown-ups are always telling kids, *If you work hard enough, you can achieve anything.* But I have my doubts. Because I've been working crazy hard to get *out* of Hebrew school and *in* to the East Bay Football League, and neither one has happened.

Yet.

CHAPTER
2

Sunday Morning

A man with a bushy white beard and big round belly stands at the front of our classroom and says, "*Boker tov, yeledim.*" That means *Good morning, children*, in Hebrew.

I've never seen the guy before. Looks exactly like Santa Claus, but that's impossible because what would Santa Claus be doing in a school full of Jewish kids?

"*Boker tov,*" I mumble along with the rest of my class. Inside my head I'm seeing the football field we passed on our way to Hebrew school. Even though the EBFL season starts next week, a bunch of kids were out there scrimmaging.

I would prefer to have my eyes poked out with a sharp stick right about now. Like if I had the option to play football with my eyes all poked out, or sit here with my eyes still in their sockets, I'd go with no eyes and football.

"My name is Rabbi Bob," Jewish Santa says. "I'm new here this year."

A small kindergartener swinging her legs in the front row gasps and shrieks, "I'm new, too!" Her dark brown curls, which are growing from her head like springs, are quivering with excitement. I almost pity her naivety. It's only a matter of time before she discovers the ugly truth about Hebrew school.

"And you are?" Rabbi Bob bends down to ask.

"My regular name is Brooke but my Hebrew name is Basha and I think everyone here should call me Little Basha because there used to be a Big Basha who's dead and I am *not* her." Her big brown eyes get even bigger when she explains this, to make sure there is no mistaking. She talks fast and has the voice of a cartoon mouse.

"You and me should stick together, then, Little Basha," Rabbi Bob says to her. She bounces in her seat and smiles enthusiastically. With her two front teeth missing, she looks even more innocent. Poor Little Basha—doesn't even know what's coming. She actually *likes* being called by her Hebrew name, which I think is the most embarrassing thing ever. Mine is Avraham and I don't let anyone use it. Ever.

Gideon in the back of the class raises his hand and Rabbi Bob calls on him.

"Hello, Rabbi Bob." Gideon tilts his head and asks, "Aren't you too old to be new?" His sandy brown, mop-like hair is mostly covering his eyes.

Everyone cranks their head to see who asked this, um, rather *bold* question. Not that I'm the king of good manners, but even I know it's rude to tell a grown-up he's old. Especially in front of an audience. But it's Gideon. Whose Hebrew name is also Gideon, which makes me feel kind of sorry for him.

We're holding our breath to see how bad Rabbi Bob's reaction will be. Is he the yelling kind, like my first-grade HST, whose face was always red and who never used an inside voice? Or is he the strict and serious kind who says things like, "Mr. Gideon, please see me after class, sir." Which is way more scary.

Rabbi Bob cups his hand at the side of his mouth and leans forward like he's going to tell us a secret. "I think what really happened," he whispers very loudly, "is Rabbi Lipschtick joined the rebel forces in another galaxy, one that is both long ago *and* far, far away."

My ears perk. Another galaxy? Long ago? Far, far away?

He looks around the class, and then for some mysterious reason he fixes his eyes on me. I have no idea why, and I don't like it. "Anyone with me on this one?" he asks.

I sort of am—curious about the Star Wars reference— but I don't want to raise my hand. After all, this is Hebrew school. And Rabbi Bob might be insane. What if this is a trick to get me to raise my hand and then he says something like, "Well, thank you for volunteering to stay after school for as long as it takes to learn the entire Torah while standing on one foot."

"I was retired myself," Rabbi Bob continues. "But I got bored staying home all day doing nothing but practicing my lightsaber maneuvers and watching ball games on TV. So I'm going to fill in for Rabbi Lipschtick for a little while, while your synagogue works to find a permanent replacement. Okey dokey?"

A few of the kids nod, but I keep my guard up. I didn't suffer through 400 days of Hebrew school to fall into some weirdo's trap.

Even if he does happen to know a little something about Star Wars.

CHAPTER
3

Monday

"Dude, what team are you on?" a kid named Damon asks. He's not asking me, of course, because I have been forbidden from fulfilling my dream of playing in the East Bay Football League. I continue eavesdropping.

"Browns," Jaxon answers.

It's the last five minutes of math and everyone is packing up to go home.

"Dude, that's harsh!" Damon snickers. "You should quit now to save face." Damon is the biggest kid in the fifth grade and has an extremely spiky faux hawk. Like he uses a gallon of hair gel to make it so spiky, and if a balloon landed on his head, it would pop. Damon also has a man voice. "My dad says there isn't, like, one single good player on that team. You're totally gonna stink-bomb this season!" Watching Damon laugh is like watching Emperor Palpatine laugh. Something just not right about it.

"You never know," a raspy voice chimes in from somewhere behind us. "Life is full of surprises." Without a doubt, it's Gideon. And I'm not going to lie—it's extremely weird to hear his voice *here*. Even though we've been in the same Hebrew school class since we were five, he's new to my regular school. Just switched over this year.

"That's what Yapa says, anyway," Gideon adds, as if anyone would know who Yapa is. His voice is like rocks tumbling in slow motion. He's awkwardly stuffing papers into his backpack. As soon as one gets in, another comes popping out. Biggest klutz in the world. I should know. He's been spilling stuff on me in Hebrew school ever since we were five.

Case in point: Three years ago, Gideon lost his balance and sent a bowl of honey down my back at Rosh Hashanah; then there was the plate of hot latkes in my lap at Chanukkah; and let's not forget the matzo ball soup at the community Passover Seder. And now I've got to worry about getting spilled on at regular school, too. I should seriously consider investing in a hazmat suit.

"I wasn't talking to you, *dill weed*," Damon says.

Damon calls everyone "dill weed." I have no idea why.

Gideon shrugs without looking up. Being called "dill weed" by one of the meanest and largest kids on the planet doesn't seem to bother him.

Truth is, nothing seems to bother Gideon. For as long as I've known him, I've never once seen him look bothered.

I keep packing up my stuff and minding my own

business (sort of, since I guess I am eavesdropping) when I hear something that could potentially change the entire course of my life.

"The new practice time is totally messed," Damon says to Jaxon.

The new practice time?

I step a little closer.

"Why?" Jaxon asks.

"I'm gonna miss *Dead Meat*. But whatever. My dad can TiVo it."

"So what are you complaining about?"

"No one should know what happens in the show before me. That's what, *dill weed*." Damon shoves Jaxon on his way out the door, even though there is definitely enough room for him to fit through the door without shoving Jaxon.

Damon is evil. But never mind. That's not what's important here.

What's important is that there is allegedly a new practice time in the football league. Which means that I might finally be able to play. But I don't want to get too excited before all the facts are in. So I need to get all the facts in. Immediately.

"Mr. S?" I ask. Mr. S is our math teacher, and the man currently holding the key to my destiny. "Would it be all right if I looked something up on the class computer? It will only take two minutes."

Mr. S nods in the direction of the computer. "Two minutes, Avery."

I race over to the open computer and type in the address for the East Bay Football League.

PLEASE NOTE: NEW PRACTICE AND GAME TIME, it says.

My hands shake as I scroll down to U10. That's my age group.

U10 TEAM PRACTICE—TUESDAYS 6:00–7:00 P.M.
U10 TEAM GAMES—SUNDAYS 12:00–1:00 P.M.

I do a quick calculation in my head.

Hebrew school ends at 6:00 on Tuesdays, and noon on Sundays. If I leave the second it lets out, I could be at the field by 6:10 on Tuesdays and 12:10 on Sundays. I've heard the coaches are pretty strict about being on time, so I'd have to make a convincing argument that they should let me on the team even though I'll be ten minutes late both days.

Not to mention I'll have to make an extra convincing argument to my parents, who are definitely not fans. "Football is a barbaric sport played by oversized thugs who enjoy giving each other concussions," they say.

But they're wrong.

I mean, I guess the crashing into each other part of football is a little barbaric, but it's also half the fun. The rest of football is skill and strategy. With eleven players on the field from each team being assigned to a bunch of different offensive and defensive positions, there are literally hundreds of possible player combinations on both sides of the ball that can be created to run plays. Figuring out how all the players on the field are going to execute a play is like getting the parts of a machine to work together. Or like mixing the right chemicals together in the right amount to get the most powerful potion. When it works, you win.

And who doesn't love to win?

I zip up my backpack and start to walk out.

"Bye, Avery," Gideon's voice startles me. I didn't even know he was still in the room. I turn around and see him struggling to zip up his backpack. I'm totally not used to seeing Gideon here. "See you at Hebrew school," he says. I wish he hadn't. It gives me that weird feeling, like the time I saw my third-grade teacher at the grocery store and she waved at me and smiled. No, thank you. Some things are meant to be kept separate. Like teachers and grocery stores. Or nuts and chocolate-chip cookies. And Hebrew school and, well, everything else.

CHAPTER
4

It's a good thing that making convincing arguments is one of my unique, highly refined talents.

With the league's first meet 'n' greet next week, which is the official start of the season, I check online to see if there's still space for one more player. There is. I can do a late registration at the meet 'n' greet, and I have enough money saved up from weekly allowances and birthdays and coins in the couch to cover the cost in case Mom and Dad say it's too expensive.

So far, so good.

For the rest of the week, I give up my science lab and don't write a single line of the next Star Wars episode. Instead, I work like mad to make air-tight arguments for my parents and the coaches in favor of letting me into the league.

By this point, Mom and Dad already know how I feel about the game, and they're not the type of people who would stand in the way of my dreams *on purpose*. Unless we're talking about how they force me to go to Hebrew school. In which case they are *exactly* the type of people who would stand in the way of my dreams on purpose.

But I've fought that battle for four solid years now, and they're just not going to budge on the issue, no matter how convincing my arguments are. So I'm taking my skills and moving on to a solid argument in favor of football.

After dinner, I do a full online demonstration of all the equipment, padding, and latest helmet technology. I point out that soccer players and basketball players don't even get this kind of protection. "So even though I have the build of a green bean," I explain, "I'll be very well protected." I tell them about how coaches know a lot more about concussions than they used to, and they're way smarter about teaching players how to tackle safely. The league even banned kickoffs, which is one of the most dangerous parts of the game.

"We just don't want to see you get clobbered," they say.

"Don't think of it as being clobbered," I answer. "Think of it as exploring a new potential."

They look at each other while not smiling. "Where does he come up with this stuff?" Mom asks. Dad shrugs.

They look back at me. I can tell they are on the fence, which is good. Great, in fact. That means at least one part of them is on my side.

"I won't get a concussion. I promise."

I know. It's kind of a hard thing to promise. But I do

anyway, hoping those will be the right words to get them completely on my side.

They look at each other, then at me, then back to each other.

They say they will think about it.

I wait extremely patiently. I make sure to be extra helpful around the house: I do not leave any articles of clothing on the floor. I wipe up every one of my pee droplets from the toilet seat. I clear all of my dishes. I take Champ for an extra walk.

The next day they have an answer. "This year," they say. "You can play for *just this year.*"

"Players get way too big after puberty," Dad says.

"Like ogres," Mom says.

"So, you're saying I can sign up for football?"

They nod, even though I can tell they wish they hadn't.

But that's a minor detail. Bottom line is: Yes!

Because the way I see it, it's better to play one year than zero years.

To get the coaches on board, I plan to show up at the meet 'n' greet thirty minutes early with all of my play books and a short speech written out on index cards about how I will be the hardest working, most dedicated player East Bay has ever seen, and that for every minute I'm late to practice (even though my tardiness is 100% out of my control and if it were up to me I would be on time, every time—or probably even early), I will stay late to run drills and put away equipment. But I probably won't need the index cards, because I've rehearsed the speech over ten thousand times in three days and have it so perfectly memorized that I can actually recite it backwards.

"I think you got it," Mom says while rubbing her temples at dinner the night before the meet 'n' greet. I'd been practicing with her all afternoon. It may have been too much for her.

When I show up at the meet 'n' greet the next day with my index cards, play books, and registration forms, there are kids everywhere on the field, tossing footballs, walking around in their football jerseys, tackling each other, and getting up and laughing. They all look like they've been doing this forever. I walk over to the registration table. My stomach is filled with butterflies. I can't believe this is actually happening.

There are two coaches at the registration table—one is wearing mirrored wrap-around sunglasses and a 49ers jersey, and the other is wearing a Chargers jersey. I hand over my registration papers to them and take a deep breath. I can feel my sweaty palms sticking to my play books and index cards. I set them down on the table. The coaches look at the stack of books and cards, then back at me.

"Hi," I begin, "my name is Avery Hirshel Green and I have wanted to play on the East Bay Football League ever since I was born." They stare at me with blank faces, which doesn't feel terribly encouraging, but I continue my speech anyway, exactly as I practiced.

"After years of being denied the opportunity because of

something called Hebrew school, which you may or may not know about, I finally have the opportunity to fulfill one of my biggest dreams because of the new EBFL practice and game times." The Chargers coach scratches his large belly. I can't see the 49ers' eyes through her wrap-around sunglasses, but I can see a twisted-up reflection of myself in them. I seriously hope that is not what I look like right now. Because if it is, they will never let me in the league.

"Thank you for making this change," I continue, trying not to look at my bizarro reflection. "Thank you so much. I don't know if I can thank you enough. Thank you! Thank you! Thank—"

"Age group?" the Chargers coach cuts me off. I didn't even get to the good part.

"U10," I say. "I'm ten years old."

"Ten?" the 49ers coach asks like she doesn't believe me. I stand up straighter and puff out my chest and stomach, trying to make myself look bigger.

I nod.

They glance over my registration form. They flip through pages on a clipboard. They look me up and down. I pull my shoulders back.

"What's the matter, kid? You don't like to eat?" the 49ers coach says.

"Go easy on him," the Chargers coach tells her. "I was a scrawny little dude myself until high school."

"Yeah, and look at you now!" the 49ers coach says. They both laugh and go back to flipping through papers. I'm not sure if I should continue my speech or not. I decide better to let them concentrate on whatever is in those very official-looking papers. I keep quiet.

"Looks like we got room on the Bears," the Chargers coach says.

The other writes something on my registration form.

"Congratulations, son," the 49ers coach says, "you're a Bear!"

I stand there frozen like an idiot. Did I hear correctly?

"That's it? I'm a … I'm a … I'm a …" I stutter.

"A Bear," the 49ers coach repeats. I remain frozen. A little breeze blows my index cards off the table. I watch as they float to the grass. The top few pages of my play book flap in the wind.

The Chargers coach hands me a piece of paper along with my stack of play books, which they never even looked at. "Here's a list of all the equipment you'll need to bring and the season schedule. Practice starts next week." He points to the far end of the field. "Bears are over there if you want to meet your coach and the other players."

"Okay, thanks," I say as I chase after my index cards.

The 49ers coach rifles through a cardboard box behind her. She tosses me a Bears jersey with the number eleven on the back. An official East Bay Football League Bears jersey. With my hands full of the index cards and my play books and the letter, I can't really catch the jersey. It lands at my feet. I awkwardly scoop it up. My feet still won't move. I didn't get the chance to finish my speech.

The 49ers coach turns to the Chargers coach and says loudly, "Why is he just standing there? Do you think he's waiting for an official draft notice?"

As I cross the field, I can feel the mass of butterflies explode from my stomach. *Who cares about the speech? I did it! I'm a Bear!* I whisper to myself.

I see a few of the Bears and the Bears' coach gathered near the end zone. I'm so excited about being on a team that I don't even care that it appears to be the same team that Damon is on.

CHAPTER

5

Tuesday Afternoon

For some reason I'm not dreading going to Hebrew school as much as I usually do. Maybe it's because I know the Bears first practice is just on the other side of it, and all I have to do is lay low and let the time pass before I can get on the field.

By the time I get to Hebrew school, everyone is already in the sanctuary, like they always are. I'm late, like I always am. I had to make a stop to the bathroom. (Dad tells me never to ignore the call of Mother Nature. I can't help it if she happens to call every Tuesday afternoon at 3:59. Dad also tells me that cleanliness is next to godliness, and since this is a place of worship, after I flush I like to give my hands a triple wash with soap, which takes time.)

I find a seat in the back. I think it would be rude to come in late and barge up to the front row.

Everyone is singing *Ma Tovu*. I'd tell you what that means

but I don't have a clue. Like practically everything in Hebrew school, the song is in Hebrew. I only understand English. Actually, that's not 100% true. Last year the class learned a few inappropriate words in Hungarian from Gideon, who learned them from his grandfather. According to my mom, Gideon's grandfather has the mouth of a drunken sailor.

When it comes to singing in Hebrew school, I have perfected the art of daydreaming about things that I'm really into while moving my lips to make it look like I'm singing. Not so much enthusiasm that I get called on to lead the class, but not so little that it looks like I'm not singing at all. This way, I stay under the radar and no one keeps me after school to actually teach me the songs. Worst nightmare.

Rabbi Bob, who has been leading this whole thing, sets down his guitar.

"*Shalom*, Avraham," he bellows across the room. "Welcome to the goodliness of our tent!"

My face turns burning hot from embarrassment. Why is he calling me Avraham? Everyone here knows to call me by my real name. And so much for an undetected sly entrance. Plus, I don't know what "the goodliness of our tent" even means.

Rabbi Bob does this big sweeping gesture with his hand along the front row and says, "Please, young Padawan, find a seat a bit closer to the action."

Aside from thinking I might die from embarrassment and working very hard not to wet myself from fear that he will make me do a solo performance of *Ma Tovu*, I am also thinking I might have hearing problems. Did he call me "young Padawan"?

I shuffle up to the front row and try not to puke. I have never been this close to the *bimah* in my life.

Rabbi Bob looks straight at me and says, "Better, that is," in a voice that sounds strangely like Yoda.

He turns to the rest of the class. Looks like I'm off the hook. For now. This Rabbi Bob seems very unpredictable. Better keep an eye on him.

"Kids," he continues in a regular voice, "as the rabbi of this synagogue, you know I have a pretty big job, don't you?"

Gideon raises his hand. He's sitting next to me, chewing on a wad of gum extremely loudly. His jaw is chomping up and down as he sputters out, "I thought you said you were temporary."

I slap my forehead. I'm afraid Gideon's mouth is going to get us all killed. He blows a ginormous bubble and when it pops, it covers the entire bottom half of his face.

"Can't wait to get rid of me, eh?" Rabbi Bob says. "You should talk to my wife … she's been stuck with me for forty years!"

After a really awkward minute of watching Gideon peel gum off his face and Rabbi Bob crack up over his own weird joke, he continues. "You're right, Gideon. I'll only be here a little while. But in that time, as your rabbi, I still have a pretty big job." He looks around the room and asks, "Does anyone here know about The Force?"

Excuse me? My heart starts racing. I sit a bit taller. But I won't raise my hand, even though I totally know about The Force.

"The mean lunch ladies at school *force* me to sit down when we're eating!" Little Basha blurts out. "Which I think is *prepotterus* because what kind of animal sits when she eats? Not horses, not rabbits, not parrots … nothing!" Little Basha's hands don't stop moving until she says, "Except for maybe chipmunks. Sometimes they sit when they eat." But then her hands start flying around again when she says, "So I know all about *force*! And I know what *prepotterus* means. It means very stupid."

Rabbi Bob chuckles. "Preposterous, indeed, Little Basha. And, yes, that is one kind of *force*. But I'm thinking of a much bigger force. I'm thinking of *The Force*."

It doesn't matter that I'm not raising my hand, because Rabbi Bob calls on me anyway.

"Avraham, you strike me as someone familiar with The Force. Am I right?" It's probably my Jar-Jar Binks t-shirt that tipped him off.

I nod, full of regret over my unfortunate wardrobe decision.

"Enlighten us, you will," he says in that Yoda voice again. Gideon twists around and gives me an enthusiastic thumbs-up. He's in the middle of blowing a bubble practically the size of his entire head and it's bobbling in my face. All of a sudden, the thing launches out of his mouth like a round, wobbly rocket and explodes on my chest, square on Jar-Jar Binks's snout.

"Yikes!" Rabbi Bob cries out. I can see Gideon was not expecting this, either.

"Sorry, Avery!" Gideon says as he leaps from his seat to help save Jar-Jar from bubble gum suffocation. He peels off the thin layer of gum that coated my shirt and pops it back in his mouth. "All better," he whispers sincerely, then stumbles back into his seat.

"A fine execution, Gideon," Rabbi Bob chuckles. He cheerfully claps his hands together and remembers what I wish he'd forgotten. "So, my young Padawans, shall we get back to it? Avraham, I believe you were just about to explain The Force to us."

There isn't anything about Star Wars I can't explain. I figure I might as well get this over with. "The Force is a mystical energy that flows through all living things and binds everything in the galaxy together," I say. "Everyone has The Force in them, but some people feel it more strongly. Those are the ones selected to become Jedis." I take a deep breath. "And can you call me by my real name? It's Avery."

"Yes, of course, Avery. And you are exactly right about The Force. Now," he continues, "I'd like you to say the exact same thing, but instead of 'The Force' say 'God.'"

I feel confused and I'm positive that my face has turned bright red, but I try to follow his instructions. "*God* is a mystical energy that flows through all living things and binds everything in the galaxy together. Everyone has *God* in them, but some people feel it more strongly. Those are the ones selected to become ... Jedis?"

Kids laugh and I feel like a complete idiot. But Rabbi Bob smiles and says, "Yes, that's right," in a very nice way that shrinks my idiot feeling.

"You may not know this, but rabbis are a lot like Jedi Masters," he says.

I find this very hard to believe, but listen anyway.

"And all of you—" he strokes his white beard— "are like my Padawans. You all have The Force inside of you. My big job is to teach you how to see it and use it. Once you know how to do that, then ..." Rabbi Bob wrinkles his forehead, squats down, and clears his throat. He finishes his sentence in Yoda's voice. "... then bring you closer to God it will."

I've got to be honest here. I don't buy it.

It's like I said—there are only three things I'm interested in getting closer to. God isn't one of them.

CHAPTER

6

Tuesday Afternoon, Later

At the end of Hebrew school, I grab Mom's hand and make her run with me out of the synagogue and all the way to the car (which was *not* optimally parked). Once we're driving, it's not long before I notice something unusual happening.

We are hitting every green light.

"I think it's a sign," I say to Mom after the fourth green light in a row.

She's still panting a little. "What's a sign?" she puffs.

"That we're getting green lights all the way from Hebrew school to the football field," I explain. "It's a sign that I'm supposed to be on the team. It's like the universe is practically rushing me to the field with all these green lights." Mom wipes her sweaty brow with a tissue. "You might want to think about working out more," I point out.

"Thanks," she grumbles. I don't think she really means it. We pass one more green light.

"Another one!" I shout. "See what I mean? It's totally a sign."

"I thought you were a man of science. What's all this talk about signs?"

"I am a man of science who happens to be stating the obvious," I explain.

It's 6:09 when we get to the field. Better than I expected. The sun is shining, not a cloud in the sky. The air is crisp.

Coach is on the far end, and all the players are running laps. Not my favorite activity, but I know it's important because it builds strength, endurance, and speed.

"Hey, Coach!" I call out as I get closer. "I'm here!"

He motions for me to start running with the team.

Damon is leading the pack. I see a few other kids from school on the team, and a bunch of kids that I don't know. Probably from other schools in the district.

I'm just about to hop in when I notice one kid trailing behind the group. Moppy brown hair flopping in his eyes, a little pudgy in the middle, running almost as if he was trapped in slow motion.

Gideon.

What's Gideon doing on the Bears? He never said anything about playing football this year. Or any years. Gideon is like the least athletic person in the world. He can barely walk across a room without somehow creating an accident, let alone actually do something that involves real coordination. Does this mean they just let *anyone* in the league? Why didn't I see him at the meet 'n' greet? And how did he get here before me?

"Hey, Avery!" he huffs as he jogs past me. "You a Bear?"

I nod, feeling a little stunned.

"Get moving, number eleven!" Coach shouts. That's me. I'm number eleven.

"Right, sorry!" I call back, and file in behind Gideon, who doesn't seem to notice that his shorts are creeping up the inside of his legs, forming a strange upside-down "v".

Gideon has fallen so far behind the group that Damon is about to lap him and is now coming up to us from behind.

"Yo, *dill weed*!" he yells to Gideon. "Outta my way!"

He speeds a little bit past us, then slows down and sticks his foot out. Of course Gideon trips over it because that is exactly what Gideon would do. If there's a trap to fall into, Gideon will 100% fall into it 100% of the time. This annoys me like crazy. It's like he's just inviting Damon to torture him and, personally, I'd prefer to stay as far away from Damon as possible.

Gideon slowly gets up to his knees, then feet. He's wiping his muddy hands on his jersey when Damon turns back. Damon's face is all twisted up like he's constipated, and his mouth is open. He makes this weird cackling kind of sound, like a demented hyena. I finally realize that this is Damon laughing while running.

"I mean *gill* weed!" he shouts. "*Gideon* ... what kind of stupid name is that?"

"It's my great-grandfather's name," Gideon answers honestly as he starts to plod along again. His cheeks are red and his thick, curly hair is sticking to the sides of his face with sweat.

By this point, though, Damon is too far ahead of us to hear Gideon. Not that he was really interested.

Luckily, for the rest of practice Damon is too busy showing off to pick on Gideon. Which is good for Gideon, for all the obvious reasons. And good for me too, because the thing is, when Damon picks on him—which he does a lot at regular school—this weird feeling comes over me like I'm supposed to do something about it. But I really, really don't want to.

It's like those old *Tom and Jerry* cartoons I watch with Bubs, where there's a little angel on one of Tom's shoulders and a little devil on the other. In my case, the little angel says, "Say something, Avery! Make Damon stop picking on him! Gideon is your friend, and friends stand up for each other!"

But the little devil says, "Pretend like you don't know Gideon! He's just a weird kid with a weird name! He's from Hebrew school, and you hate Hebrew school! Plus, Gideon is a Damon-magnet! And you hate Damon! The less you have to do with Gideon, the better!"

Thinking about this stuff bums me out.

It's my first official day of being on the Bears and we hit every green light. The sun is shining, not a cloud in the sky. The air is crisp.

I'm not going to let anything bum me out.

"Gideon! *Shalom!*" a holler comes from the side of the field. I look up and see a man in a track suit walking two dogs—one very huge and one very small—wildly waving his hands. "Gideon! Hi! Over here!" I look up and squint.

No, this isn't happening.

It's Rabbi Bob. Is he following me or something?

I quickly spin on my heels so that my back is facing him. Meanwhile, Gideon answers Rabbi Bob's call. He waves back equally wildly and shouts, "Hey, Rabbi Bob!" loud enough for everyone to hear. I want to hide under a rock and disappear, even though Rabbi Bob hasn't seen me.

I sigh with relief when he walks away with his dogs. Gideon jogs back to practice. "That was Rabbi Bob out there," he pants. "Did you see him?"

I shake my head and run back to my drill station. I'm not going to let anything bum me out.

CHAPTER

7

Sunday Morning

It's perfect outside, again. Seventy-two degrees, not a cloud in the sky, light breeze. And how do I get to enjoy this perfect morning? Back inside of an old stuffy synagogue doing nothing but sitting.

"Have you heard of sitting disease?" I ask Mom on the way to Hebrew school.

She doesn't answer.

"It's a real thing, you know. My PE teacher taught us all about it. Sitting disease is what's happening in the modern world because people sit too much. Our muscles are turning to goo because we don't use them enough. That's the disease."

"I thought you hated PE now that you have to learn ballroom dancing," she replies.

"That's beside the point, Mom. This is about sitting disease, and how I'm going to catch it if I spend too much time sitting and not enough time running around in the fresh air exercising my heart, lungs, and muscles. Did you know physical activity is proven to make you smarter, too?"

"You don't say." Mom sounds unimpressed.

I look out the window and sigh loudly as we pass the football field. "There's a lot of sitting in Hebrew school," I tell her. "*A lot.*"

"You ever heard the expression *Give a man a finger and he takes the whole hand?*" she asks.

"Does this have anything to do with sitting disease?"

"No. It has to do with a kid who convinced the coaches *and* his parents—against their better judgment, I might add—concussions are a serious problem!—to let him play football this year, and still he wants to *kvetch* about going to Hebrew school."

I decide at this point it's better for me to keep quiet. I've only heard the concussions speech about a thousand times since they agreed to let me sign up, and I'm not sure I'm up for 1,001. *One injury, young man, and you're off the team. Understood?* Seems like it would be bad luck to hear that again before our first game of the season this afternoon.

When we get to the synagogue, I drag myself up the stairs. It takes me an extra-long time, and I'm pretty sure this is because my muscles are turning to goo. Once I reach the top, I hear a very strange noise coming from inside the sanctuary. A high-pitched whining noise, like a ghost from a haunted house.

I pick up the pace.

Once inside, I see Rabbi Bob on the *bimah*, standing in front of a narrow wooden boxy thing on a stand. He's waving his hands in front of two metal antennas coming out of it, but he's not touching anything. I have no idea how, but it seems like he's making the spooky sound with his hands.

Little Basha is on her feet in the front row doing a ghosty, spaghetti noodle dance to the weird tune.

"*Boker tov*, Avery," he belts out over the loud noise. "A good day to come to Hebrew school," he says, focusing on his hands as they move slowly around the air in front of the antennas. The high-pitched noise sounds like it's dipping up and down to the same rhythm as his hand motions. "Got the feeling last week that you were doubtful about The Force that lives in each of us. Brought in one of my favorite toys this week to prove you wrong."

I am so confused. Am I in the right place? I look around. This is Hebrew school, right?

"As you can see, I'm not touching this instrument. And yet … listen!" Rabbi Bob seems very proud of himself. "It's called a Theremin, by the way. Invented by a Russian scientist in the 1920s. And it uses the energy—the *force*, you might say—coming from my hands to pick up signals in the antennas. One controls the volume—" Rabbi Bob demonstrates by moving one hand to make the sound louder and quieter— "and one controls the pitch." He moves the other hand to make the sound higher and lower.

Rabbi Bob stops waving his hands and the sound stops.

Everyone in the room looks kind of shocked, except for Gideon in the front row, who I see is staring off into space while picking his nose, and Rabbi Bob, who has a suspicious grin on his face. "I'd like to dedicate this next tune to my young Padawan friend, Avery Green, who does not yet recognize The Force within himself."

My stomach drops to my knees. Why does Rabbi Bob keep calling me out? If anyone should be called out, it's Gideon, who is right now eating his own boogers.

Rabbi Bob does a big arm stretch and knee bend, then cracks his knuckles before beginning the song. It takes me exactly two seconds to recognize it. The theme song from Star Wars.

And he plays it perfectly.

•

Aside from the Jewish-Santa-Theremin-Star-Wars thing, the rest of Hebrew school goes basically the same as always.

Kids are released from the sanctuary into the classrooms which are divided into two groups: little kids and big kids. There are only ten of us. Not enough to make a separate class for each grade. That's because there are hardly any Jewish people in our town.

"You should at least have a few friends who celebrate the same holidays as you," Dad says.

"Not everyone in the whole world celebrates Christmas," Mom says.

"Not everyone in the whole world celebrates Diwali, either, but you don't see Akira's parents forcing her to go to Hindu school," I argue. Akira is from India and she's the only other kid in my grade at regular school who doesn't celebrate Christmas. Well, until Gideon came this year.

"Too bad you don't have Akira's parents," they tell me.

I'm in the big kids group. They call us the Maccabi Tel Aviv. The little kids are called the Maccabi Haifa. These are famous soccer teams in Israel. Except in Israel "soccer" is called *kadur-regel*, which translates to "football." I actually like our class names, even though I don't understand why we have them. We never actually play soccer. Or football.

What we do actually do is open up our Hebrew *aleph-bet* books and write the same Hebrew letters over and over a million times, recite the same prayers over and over also a million times, and learn Torah stories about people who lived in the desert a million years ago.

I know. Our species of humans didn't live a million years ago. But they did live two hundred thousand years ago, which is way longer than six thousand years ago, which is what it says in the Torah. The Torah is the Jewish bible, which tries to make us believe that Adam and Eve were the first humans and that God created them six thousand years ago, give or take a few years. Which is why I have a hard time getting into the Torah. How am I supposed to get into a book that doesn't even get the facts straight?

The teacher for the Maccabi Tel Aviv is called Morah Neetza. I think *morah* is what you're supposed to call teachers in Hebrew. Either that, or every teacher I've ever had in Hebrew school has the first name Morah.

Morah Neetza has hair like a maroon-colored sponge and wears jewelry that makes a lot of noise. She's from Israel, where it's always warm, which basically means if it's under sixty-five degrees outside she will wear a winter coat, plus a hat, scarf, and mittens, and she can't pronounce the *th* sound—which comes out as either a *z* or a *t*—or the *h* sound at the beginning of words, which just gets forgotten altogether. Morah Neetza doesn't smile much, but I wouldn't exactly say she's mean. It's more like no one ever told her she was allowed to smile. "When I was in school," she tells us, "zere were fifty-two children in a class and we weren't allowed to speak."

Morah Neetza also wears platform sneakers covered in rhinestones and puffy paint. This makes me wonder if she's always as serious as she looks.

"*Yeledim*, children," Morah Neetza starts, "who can tell me what *very* important Jewish 'oliday is right around ze corner?"

Nobody raises a hand.

"Anyone? Let's tink. A very important Jewish 'oliday zat comes every fall right about ze time of ze *new* school *year*." She says *new* and *year* louder and slower. "Hmmm?" she says.

Gideon raises his hand but Morah Neetza pretends not to notice, which is hard with only five students. Teachers always seem a little scared to call on Gideon. But eventually, she has to call on him. "Yes, Gideon, what 'oliday is just around ze corner?"

"Um, Halloween?" he says.

Morah Neetza sighs. "*Jewish* 'oliday, Gideon. *Jew-ish*."

Gideon shrugs his shoulders and chews on the little pink eraser at the top of his chewed-up pencil.

"Children, it's Rosh Hashanah. Ze Jewish new year. And it comes every fall. Now—" she claps her hands together and her zillion bracelets jingle like crazy— "who can tell me why it's so important? What makes Rosh Hashanah so *special*?"

Gideon raises his hand again but Morah Neetza rushes in to answer her own question. "On Rosh Hashanah we reflect on our deeds from ze past year. We tink about our mistakes. We tink about what we should 'ave done differently. And zen we ask for forgiveness—from ourselves, from uh-zers, and, most importantly, from God. So …" Morah Neetza digs into her spongy hair and gives her scalp a little scratch, "… in preparation for zis 'oly day, today we are going to begin a very meaningful reflection of ze past year."

Morah Neetza gets a stack of paper.

"I make mistakes. You make mistakes. We are 'uman, and 'umans sometimes act like pigs, right?" She begins to pass out the paper and mumbles, "I should know. I have an ex-'usband."

Morah Neetza's bracelets jingle some more. "Your assignment is to tink of all ze mistakes zat you made in ze past year and write zem down. What are you sorry for? I want a big list from everybody. *Beseder?* Okay?"

Kids start scribbling away, except for Gideon, who has

started a coughing fit. By the look of his nubby pencil, I believe he has swallowed the little pink eraser.

"Gideon, what's ze problem?" Morah Neetza asks.

He waves his hand and spouts out between coughs, "Don't … worry … I … got … it …"

Gideon barks a huge final cough and the little pink eraser comes flying out. It soars through the air in slow motion and lands right in my lap. I watch as it rolls down my thigh, leaving a snail trail of mucus down my leg.

Seriously, where's a hazmat suit when you need one?

The pink blob falls at my feet. There is no way I am going to touch that.

Morah Neetza walks over in her sparkly platform sneakers. She pulls a crumpled tissue out from her bosom like she's got a whole stash of them in her bra. "Zis is not a big deal, Avery," she scolds. "You want a big deal? Try sleeping in ze mud for six weeks in ze Israeli army wiz nuh-zing to eat but boiled eggs and frozen schnitzel." She scoops the blob up with her tissue. "You don't want to know ze stuff I picked up in ze army." She then slides a blank piece of paper on my desk. "Time for work," she says.

I look at it.

It stares back at me.

I have no idea what to write. The only thing I'm sorry about is that I have to waste a sunny morning sitting in this crummy room writing about things I'm sorry about.

Luckily, Mother Nature comes to call. I raise my hand and ask, "May I go to the bathroom?"

Morah Neetza replies, "When I was in school, we didn't even 'ave a bazroom. We 'eld it in. Zat's what we did. For nine hours, we 'eld it."

I'm not sure if she's saying yes or no.

Morah Neetza picks at a little piece of food stuck in her teeth with her bright orange fingernails and looks at me with a blank stare. "Make it queeck, Avery. We're going to share our ideas in two minutes."

Sharing our ideas? As if doing this assignment wasn't bad enough, she wants us to share?

I dash out of the room. On the way to the bathroom, my brain shifts into high gear to come up with something to share because I'm pretty sure Morah Neetza isn't going to appreciate me being sorry for missing football.

I was thinking: *Just make something up, like tell her you're sorry that you let Champ poop on the neighbor's lawn.* But then I thought about something that I actually am sorry about. I should have stood up for Gideon at practice on Tuesday when Damon teased and tripped him.

Something heavy sinks into my stomach. It's not a nice feeling.

I'm in the middle of this guilt-fest when I suddenly notice a strange moving light coming from Rabbi Bob's office. It's bright red and glowing from the crack in the doorway. The door is slightly opened.

I step a bit closer to the door to make sure I'm not hallucinating.

I can say this: if I *am* hallucinating, then my hallucination includes sound, because in addition to the glowing red light, I also hear a deep zapping noise.

I kneel down to get a closer look and listen.

Maybe it's the Theremin, I guess, even though it doesn't sound anything like what he played earlier in the sanctuary. And the Theremin didn't glow red.

I crawl up to the door and put my finger where the light is glowing. It stops moving.

My shoulder accidently knocks the door. Before I know it, Rabbi Bob kneels down on his hands and knees on the other side of the door. We are eye to eye.

"Something I can help you with, Avery?" he whispers through the crack.

I jump back and land on my butt. "Um, no, no, thanks," I stammer as I do a backwards crab crawl away from his door. "All good here!"

I scramble to my feet and run to the bathroom.

Scared? Maybe. A little.

I mean, what if Rabbi Bob was spying on me at practice last week and knows that I haven't been a good friend to a fellow Hebrew school inmate and the red light is some sort of torture machine that is going to make me admit that I was wrong and my punishment will be to stay longer at Hebrew school and therefore have to quit the Bears?

Rabbi Bob *is* strange.

But how strange? And strange how?

And what is up with that coo-coo-banana-split red light?

CHAPTER

Sunday Afternoon, First Game of the Season

I missed warm-up on account of Hebrew school, but
that's okay. I did twenty pushups, jogged in place for four
minutes, and tackled Champ very carefully when I woke up
this morning to keep on top of this whole sitting disease
thing, which Hebrew school will definitely give me if I'm
not careful. And which I definitely cannot afford to get
now that I'm on the Bears.

When I get to the field, all the players are huddled around
Coach.

Gideon sees me coming and opens up the circle to
squeeze me in.

Seriously, how does that kid get here before me? I swear
I left Hebrew school before him *and* we had a good parking
space this time.

"Hey, Avery," he whispers as I step into the huddle.

Gideon looks as unnatural in his full uniform as a chipmunk in a sombrero.

I give him a nod hello but focus all my attention on Coach, who is holding a small whiteboard covered in Xs, Os, and arrows. I can see right away it's a basic "I" formation—two wide receivers, two running backs, and one tight end. I'm best at being a wide receiver. That's because I'm small and agile and I can dart around the bigger guys. I also have amazing accuracy for catching. It's like I can see exactly where a pass is going to land and I can calculate how to get there without getting crushed. This will be the first time I get to test my skills on a real team, with a real coach, in a real uniform, against real opponents.

Talk about a dream come true.

Coach puts his hand in the middle of the huddle and all the players put their hands on top of his. "1, 2, 3 … Go, Bears!" everyone chants, then breaks apart.

Since I arrived late—and I'm a rookie—I won't be one of the starting players. That's okay. I can get a better sense of the field and the other team's weak spots from the bench. I brought my play book to take notes, too. We're up against the Vikings this week.

I get settled on the bench and look up from my play book. At the far end of the field, I see a man walking two dogs—one very huge and one very small. My stomach wads up into a hot, tangled mess. Rabbi Bob is spying on me, isn't he? I hunch over and hide my face into my play book until I see the figures of Rabbi Bob and his dogs disappear into the distance.

I take a deep breath and shake it off. Hebrew school has kept me away from football long enough.

•

Thirty-five minutes into the game and it's pretty clear that the Vikings know what they're doing. We're down by fifteen points and they have the ball. Coach hasn't put me in yet, but that's probably because I'm the new kid and he doesn't know what I can do. Too risky when we're down.

I'm taking notes like mad, though. My play book is practically smoking.

Not surprisingly, Damon—who is the size of a tank—is the defensive lineman. He's good at it, too.

But not as good as his father thinks. Or at least I'm 99.9% sure the man in the Bears hoodie who's been coaching Damon extremely loudly from the stands is his father. Damon looks like a shrunken clone of the guy, down to the brick-wall shoulders, permanently angry eyebrows, and deathly spiky faux hawk.

"TAKE HIM DOWN, SON!" he shouts. Yep, it's Damon's dad. "HE'S HALF YOUR SIZE! SHOW THEM WHO'S BOSS!" he barks, as if he's the coach and Damon is the only player. He's also been recording the entire game on his phone.

Unfortunately, Damon's dad is standing right next to my

parents, who are sitting on the bleachers looking terrified and fanning away smoke blowing in their faces coming from an old man sitting on the other side of them. The old man is wearing a full-on Russian fur hat with the flaps tied under his chin, puffing away on a cigar like he never heard the news that smoking will kill him.

Mom and Dad give me a nervous wave. It looks like a very unpleasant sandwich that they've been squeezed into.

I'm wishing Mom and Dad were having a better experience. They already think it's a barbaric sport, and Damon's dad isn't doing much to change their minds about that. I just hope all that second-hand smoke doesn't cloud their judgment and cause them to change their minds about letting me play.

But there will be more chances for them to see how great football is. Right? For now, I've got to concentrate on taking notes. Because if we go up against the Vikings again this year, I want us to be more prepared than …

Oh, man. Vikings just scored another touchdown.

"Gideon … Avery … last five minutes! You're up!" Coach shouts as he throws down his clipboard. He takes off his Bears cap and scratches the top of his balding head. He's not making eye contact with anyone. Coaches never make eye contact when they know they've been defeated. It's something I've noticed from years of observation.

Gideon and I look at each other. I can tell he's as

surprised as me. This is the first time he's going in the game, too.

"Damon … Ethan … come on out!" Coach shouts and waves his hands for Damon and Ethan, who is the other wide receiver, to come out. Apparently Gideon is going to be a lineman. He's pretty big, so it makes sense from Coach's point of view. But if he knew Gideon the way I do, he'd probably think twice.

Once, in second grade, Gideon accidentally crushed a roly-poly bug he found in the dirt in front of the synagogue. He spent the rest of the afternoon crying with the dead bug on his desk. The next time I saw him at Hebrew school he was dressed in black carrying an empty match box decorated as a coffin.

I never knew a bug funeral could be such an emotional experience.

But that's Gideon. And here he is now, jogging onto the field as an offensive lineman against the Vikings for the next five minutes.

As a man of science, even I have the urge to say a little prayer.

"YOU GOTTA BE KIDDING ME!" Damon's dad shouts from the stands. "YOU ON A SUICIDE MISSION OR SOMETHING, COACH? DAMON'S THE ONLY DECENT PLAYER YOU GOT!" For a brief moment, I actually feel a teensy bit sorry for Damon because, well, that can't be good having your dad embarrass you like that in front of everyone. But then I overhear Damon dig into Gideon as they switch places.

"Good luck getting killed, *gill weed*. Ya *loser*."

I feel about as sorry for Damon as I do for Emperor Palpatine.

CHAPTER

9

Tuesday

Ever since last Sunday's massive upset—which became a complete nightmare in the last five minutes after Gideon picked up a loose fumble and ran it in the *wrong direction*—I've needed to spend a lot of time in my science lab. When things aren't going very well, that's usually where I go. That also happens to be where I go when things *are* going very well. I pretty much love it down there.

Mom calls it my happy place. Dad made a sign that says *BEWARE: MAD SCIENTIST AT WORK* and hung it on the door to my lab. They usually let me spend as much time as I want down there, as long as I follow the rules.

1. Always wear protective eyewear.
2. No matches.
3. Open window when odors become offensive.
4. Clean up after yourself.

They also do a pretty good job helping me keep it stocked with useful supplies. They were willing to eat tuna fish at every meal for a whole week when I was working on Potion #17. And they didn't tell me I was crazy the time I spent four straight hours perfecting my recipe for elephant toothpaste. Or yell at me when the elephant toothpaste was so explosive that I needed a ladder to scrape it off the ceiling.

They even let me go to yard sales in search of old, cheap electronics that I can take apart. I think it was after I dissected their toaster oven that we started doing that.

Or maybe it was the phone.

Or the clock radio.

Never mind. The point is that my lab is my haven where I get to be in control of how things go. It's where I started to feel less miserable and defeated after our miserable defeat by the Vikings.

Now that it's Tuesday, I'm feeling more optimistic. More determined. I remember that I've got a mystery to solve. Rabbi Bob may think that he's spying on me. But he's dead wrong. I'm spying on him.

The Mission: Reveal the mystery of Rabbi Bob's coo-coo-banana-split red light.

The Agent: Avery Green, Man of Science, Revealer of Mysteries.

•

"Can you step on it, Mom? I don't want to be late for Hebrew school."

Mom pinches me. Hard.

"Ouch!" I yelp. "What was that for?"

"I've never seen you in a hurry to get to Hebrew school. Just wanted to make sure that I'm not dreaming."

"Aren't you supposed to pinch *yourself* to make sure you're not dreaming?"

"Probably. But I thought it would be more fun to pinch you."

"Very funny," I reply. "And no, you're not dreaming. I'm working on kind of a cool project at the synagogue and I don't want to be late is all."

Mom smiles.

"Don't get any weird ideas that I suddenly like Hebrew school, because I don't," I explain. "Definitely hate it as much as always. Okay?"

"Okay with me as long as you go," Mom chirps.

•

When I enter the synagogue, the little Maccabi Haifas are gathered around Gideon in the lobby. He's teaching them how to burp the *alef-bet*. It's a thing he does every year with the new kids, who are totally mesmerized.

"… *vav, zion, chet, tet, yud* …" Gideon burps proudly. I have to admit, it's pretty impressive. It's actually helped me memorize my Hebrew letters. "… *koof, reish, shin, tav!*" he finishes and takes a bow.

"Wow!" Little Basha squeals, "that is so amazing! Will you teach me how to burp the alfalfa bits?"

Gideon smiles and burps the words, "Of course I will, Little Basha."

Little Basha jumps up and down and rams into Gideon's belly to give him a massive hug. Her twiggy arms barely reach around his middle.

"*Tov, yeledim*, ze burping show is over," Morah Neetza says sternly. She rolls her eyes and scratches her head through her spongy hair. "Tank you, Gideon. Such a gift," she says dryly.

"You're welcome," Gideon burps.

Morah Neetza ushers us into the sanctuary. Rabbi Bob is on the *bimah*. No Theremin this time. No instruments at all, in fact, not even his guitar. Just a big ol' ram's horn.

Without saying a word, Rabbi Bob lifts the long, curly ram's horn to his mouth. He takes a huge breath and his round belly gets even rounder. He wraps his lips around the small end of the ram's horn and blows as hard as he can.

Nothing happens.

He does it again, and still nothing happens.

Rabbi Bob scratches his head. He turns the ram's horn around in his hands. "Was I supposed to charge this thing?" he wonders out loud. "Okay, one more try, and if it doesn't work, I'm taking it straight back to the shyster ram who sold it to me."

Rabbi Bob takes his deepest breath yet, squeezes his eyes

shut, puffs his cheeks like a squirrel stuffed with nuts, and blows hard into the ram's horn.

"TOOOOOT!" the thing blasts. We all jump back and cover our ears. "TOOOOT TOOOOT!"

"Good," Rabbi Bob says. "Now that you're all awake, I can give you your first homework assignment."

A few kids grumble. I know exactly how they feel. It's bad enough that we have homework for regular school. Now we have homework for Hebrew school?

Not that I was a fan of Rabbi Lipschtick, but at least he never gave us homework.

"Have any of you ever played a name game?" Rabbi Bob asks. "Like an ice-breaker—something to help people in a group get to know each other better."

Little Basha begins to sing and snap her fingers. "Basha, Basha, fofasha, me my momasha ... Basha!" She beams and wiggles in her seat. "Circle time. Preschool. Good name game," she explains.

No one else says a word. Probably because we are too confused by Little Basha's song and too angry about a homework assignment to speak.

"Ah, I see," Rabbi Bob says. "With the refreshing exception of Little Basha, you all appear to be the silent type. Very well, then, let me get straight to it. Your first assignment is to ask your parents how they chose your Hebrew name."

Rabbi Bob hands each of us a paper with lots of questions we're supposed to ask our parents. He continues, "Maybe you were named after someone. Maybe your name has a special meaning. Maybe they just liked the sound of it, like Basha, Basha, fofasha, me my momasha … Basha! Whatever the reason, find out. Come back with your stories and we'll begin to share them."

Rabbi Bob smiles, which I find very irritating under the circumstances.

"Once we know ourselves," he says, "we can get to know each other."

Again, angry silence.

"Now go forth and learn!" he cries out, and flicks us away with the shake of his hands.

●

"May I go to the bathroom, please?" I ask Morah Neetza ten minutes into the class. That's about as long as I can wait before commencing Operation Weird Red Light.

"Tell your muh-zer to take you to ze doctor, Avery," Morah Neetza answers. "I don't like how you always have to make pee-pee."

I'm not sure if that's a yes or a no.

Morah Neetza's bracelets jingle as she shoos me out. "Make it queeck!"

I race out of the room but slow down as soon as I approach Rabbi Bob's office. There is no red light coming from his door. I quietly step closer. No sound either. The room is dark. Even though I haven't technically done anything wrong, I feel kind of nervous, like I have.

All of a sudden, I hear a familiar deep zapping noise. A beam of bright red light shoots out from the dark crack under the door. My heart starts racing and my palms get all sweaty. The door creaks open wider and a hand crawls out. A finger attached to the hand calls me in. My face gets burning hot and my heart feels like it's going to explode out of my chest.

The finger curls again and again, urging me to step inside Rabbi Bob's office.

I take a deep breath and walk into the dark room with the deep zapping sound and mysterious red light. After all, this is my mission.

The buzzing and the light intensify. It takes my eyes a moment to adjust. I blink a few times and look up to find Rabbi Bob standing before me like a statue.

In his hands, a red lightsaber.

"Ever seen one of these?" he asks.

•

You know how people in movies faint when something shocking happens? I always thought that was just in the movies.

I'm only ten years old but I've now lived long enough to say with authority that it's not just in the movies.

Because the next thing I remember after Rabbi Bob asking me, "Ever seen one of these?" is waking up on the sofa in the lobby of the synagogue with Gideon in my face.

"You okay, Avery?" he asks. His warm breath smells like a Mexican restaurant.

I blink a few times to get my eyes focused.

"Um, I think so." I look up.

Rabbi Bob and Morah Neetza are hovering over me. Rabbi Bob has a suspicious smile on his face, like he knows what happened but he isn't going to tell anyone. Morah Neetza is fanning a piece of paper over my face. Her bracelets are jangling very, very loudly. I think my head will pop if she keeps going like this.

"What happened?" I ask.

"You fainted, little man. But you're okay," Rabbi Bob says.

"I fainted once," Gideon says. "It was a hot day and I was covered in *a lot* of fur."

There is a moment of silence. Sometimes it's hard to know what to say after Gideon speaks.

"The ice water saved me," he says. He walks over to the water bubbler and comes back shuffling slowly so that he doesn't spill the overfilled little cup. I can see from my sideways position on the couch that his shoelaces are untied, dragging behind him like loose spaghetti. "Here, this will help," he says, reaching toward me with the cup. He's right at the foot of the sofa when his long shoelace gets caught under his final step. He loses balance and—yes, of course!—spills the ice-cold water directly on my face.

"Oof!" he cries.

"Whoa, boy!" Rabbi Bob cries.

"*Oy vey ist mir*," Morah Neetza mumbles.

"Oh, I'm so sorry, Avery! Are you okay?" Gideon asks as he uses the bottom of his shirt to mop up my face.

"I'm fine," I say truthfully. "It actually feels kind of good." The icy splash makes me feel a little less groggy. I sit up.

"You're too skinny," Morah Neetza offers as she roughly dabs at my neck with scratchy paper towels. "You don't eat enough! Zis is why you faint! Look at you, like a skeleton! 'Ere—" Morah Neetza shoves a pita sandwich in my face. "Eat!"

I take a look at the soggy pita with hummus crusted at the edges and stuffed with floppy cucumbers and my stomach turns. "No, thanks," I say.

"You see what I mean!" Morah Neetza cries. "Ze boy doesn't eat! Zis is why he faints!"

The Maccabi Haifa and Maccabi Tel Aviv kids poke their heads out the classroom doors.

"I'll take that sandwich if Avery doesn't want it," Gideon says calmly.

Rabbi Bob takes the sandwich from Morah Neetza. "Thank you, Morah Neetza. You, too, Gideon. How about I hold on to the sandwich for Avery? You go ahead and get back to your class," Rabbi Bob suggests. "I'll take care of Avery until his mom comes."

Morah Neetza jingles away with Gideon trailing behind her. He turns back to say, "Hope you feel better soon, Avery."

Once they're back in the classroom, Rabbi Bob sits on the sofa by my feet and whispers, "I'm guessing that's the first lightsaber you've seen in real life."

I nod my head slowly.

"Well, you come back on Sunday and I'll show you how to use it. Okay?"

My head keeps nodding.

CHAPTER
10

Tuesday, Later

"Morah Neetza mentioned that Avery hadn't eaten much today," Rabbi Bob says to my mom when she comes to pick me up early. "Must have been a case of low blood sugar and a little dehydration." Rabbi Bob looks at me and winks. "Happens to the best of us. A little food and something to drink and I'm sure he'll be fine."

Mom brushes my hair to the side. "Getting this kid to eat can be a real chore," she says, "but maybe a stop at the Burger Ranch will get him back upright."

The Burger Ranch. Only the best burgers in the world. And they'll make a milk shake out of any of their sixty-two flavors, including Jelly Bean Dream, which is a perfect blend of jelly beans and cotton-candy-flavored ice cream. It's my favorite mostly because it's the only one my parents won't steal from me for a so-called sip, but which is more like half the shake. They think Jelly Bean

Dream should be against the law. This makes me love it even more.

"What do you think, Avery? Burger Ranch sound good for an early dinner?"

•

"Aside from fainting, how was Hebrew school today?" Mom asks me over a plate of fries.

"Same," I reply with a mouth full of burger. "Except that we have an assignment. I'm supposed to ask you how you picked my Hebrew name."

"Well that sounds nice!" Mom says a little too cheerfully. "As you know, you're named after my grandfather, Avraham Hirshel. That's how you got to be Avery Hirshel Green."

She's right. That much I knew.

"Did I ever show you the book I made about Avraham?" I shake my head.

"Tonight, let's do that."

"Okay," I reply, stuffing in the last bite of perfect burger. I look at my watch. It's 5:48.

"If we leave now, I can get to practice on time," I say.

"Ah, honey," Mom says, "are you sure you're up for football today? You did faint this afternoon, you know. Don't you think it would be wiser to give your body a chance to rest?"

I slurp the last of my beautiful blue milkshake. A chunk of jelly bean gets stuck in my straw, but no worries. I've been in this situation before. I blow into my straw as hard as I can and the pink chunk comes hurling out into my cup.

"Not really," I say chewing on the last delicious morsel of my shake. "In fact, I think football will make me feel even better. You know, get the blood flowing to my brain again," I reason. "You ever heard of sitting disease?" I ask.

Mom looks at me without saying a word.

"I heard fainting is a common sign that a person is developing sitting disease. The only way to overcome the disease is to do vigorous athletic things."

"Let me guess," Mom says. "Like play football?"

"You got it!" I say.

•

Coach is working us hard after Sunday's epic disaster. Ethan, the other wide receiver, and I are running quick feet explosion drills around cones. Good for developing core and leg strength, and agility. Coach has got the quarterbacks running sideways through a rope ladder on the grass. The linesmen are on all fours in rows facing each other doing pad drills. Each time Coach blows the whistle, they lift up and crash their shoulder pads into each other.

Everything seems to be going great. The whole team—with the exception of Gideon, who still occasionally runs the wrong way—is getting stronger and preparing for victory and vanquishing sitting disease. But then, out of nowhere, I hear a scream. It's a high-pitched howl, like a bird who's been shot with a poison dart. Everyone turns to see what happened. Gideon is curled up on the ground and Damon is very suspiciously walking away. He's the only one not staring at Gideon. Which makes him the number one suspect.

That, and he's evil.

Coach runs up to Gideon. He wraps his arms under Gideon and lifts him up. They hobble over to the bench, where Coach keeps a water jug and first-aid kit. He takes off Gideon's helmet and we hear that high-pitched howl again. Blood is streaming from Gideon's face.

The little angel on my shoulder is saying, "What are you waiting for? Help Gideon! Remember how he helped you after you fainted? You can see he's hurt! Don't just stand there!"

But the little devil is saying the opposite. "Helped you?! That klutz spilled ice-cold water on your face! Don't worry about Gideon. Besides, Coach is taking care of him. You'll just get in the way."

Coach presses an ice pack over Gideon's nose and sits him down on the bench. Then he blows the whistle at the rest of us. "Drills!" he snaps.

All the guys straggle back to the drills they were doing. I stay behind and watch as Gideon scrunches his face in agony. Coach examines his nose, which has become huge and red. But at least he's stopped the howling noise.

"How about when I press here?" Coach asks. "That okay?"

I can tell Gideon is fighting back tears. "Not too bad," he says. He looks up and sees me. He gives a weak wave. "Hey, Avery." His voice is shaky and sounds stuffed up, like he has a bad cold.

Coach gives me a hard look. "You waiting for a written invitation, Avery? You heard me. Get back to work."

The little angel wants me to tell Coach that Gideon is my friend, and to stay with him. But the little devil wants me to keep quiet and follow Coach's orders.

Stick around if you want to stink by association! the little devil cackles. *Gideon is fine anyway. He's just being dramatic.*

His nose is swollen to the size of a bagel, the little angel argues back. *You call that being dramatic?*

I'm standing there like an idiot as the little devil and the little angel on my shoulders bicker at each other. Coach shakes his head at me. "You want a repeat of last Sunday?" he barks.

I think the little devil is afraid of Coach. I turn away and jog over to the drill area.

In the distance, I see the silhouette of a man walking two dogs—one very huge and one very small.

As a man of science, I remind myself that I do not believe in omens.

•

When we get home, Mom brings down the scrap book she made about her grandfather, Avraham. I'm still feeling weird about how practice went today. I can tell Mom is super-excited to show me her book. She goes through every page so slowly that I start to wonder if *I'll* be the grandfather by the time she gets to the end. I write everything down on the paper Rabbi Bob gave us, even though my mind keeps wandering.

Eventually she says, "And that's the story of your great-grandfather, and your name!" She looks very pleased with herself.

"Nice," I say, trying to be polite. I wonder if Gideon is okay. I mean, just because he's basically a disaster on the football field doesn't mean he deserves to have his nose broken, right? If anyone deserves to have a broken nose, it's Damon, for being so evil.

CHAPTER

11

Sunday Morning

This may be the craziest thing I've ever said, but I'm actually looking forward to Hebrew school today.

Is this what an identity crisis feels like?

Nah.

This is what it feels like on the day I discover the truth about Rabbi Bob. And the day he actually lets me use his 100% bona fide, certified, completely real lightsaber and I am not going to faint.

Also, I kind of want to find out how Gideon's face is doing, and if it still looks like a bagel is sitting on it.

Rabbi Bob is waiting for us when we get to the sanctuary.

"*Shalom*, young Padawans," he says. "Are you ready to get to know one another?"

Little Basha bounces in her seat and squeals, "Y.E.S. spells yes!"

No one else answers.

"Tough crowd." Rabbi Bob chuckles. "But let's see if we can crack through this hard exterior, shall we?"

"Y.E.S. spells yes!" Little Basha squeals again.

Silence from the rest of us.

Rabbi Bob rubs his hands together like he's about to announce something exciting.

"At the start of each class," he says, "we're going to put one of you in the hot seat." He points to a stool on the *bimah*. "And you will tell us all about your name."

My only thought is: Please don't start with the As.

"Starting with the As …" he says, very enthusiastically drumming on his legs. "… Can we get a drum roll please?"

Kids weakly join him in the "drum roll," except for Little Basha, who is practically drumming herself off the bench.

"First up is …"

My stomach does a full somersault because I know exactly where this is going.

"… Avery!"

Zachary. Why couldn't my parents have named me Zachary?

"Step right up, Avery!"

Gideon, whose nose looks more like half a bagel today, whispers, "You got this, Avery!" as I pass by.

I slowly drag myself up to the stool. I take the folded paper with everything Mom told me out of my pocket.

"They named me after my great-grandfather, Avraham Hirshel," I start. "He was my mom's grandfather. My whole name is Avery Hirshel Green."

Rabbi Bob nods, encouraging me to say more.

"He was born in Belgium in 1912. Which is very easy for me to remember because the number twelve also happens to be Tom Brady's jersey number. Only the best quarterback of all time."

"Even the sages couldn't argue with that," Rabbi Bob says.

"His family was in the diamond business. My mom says Jewish people in Europe didn't have a lot of choices for work, but they were allowed to do diamond trading."

"Yes," Rabbi Bob says, "that's correct."

"She said her family had it pretty good in Belgium until the Nazis came to power. She said that the Nazis thought the world would be a better place without Jews in it."

The world would be a better place without Jews in it? Saying that out loud in a room with a bunch of Jewish kids suddenly sounds weird. My face feels hot. I look up and Gideon is shaking his head *No.* I swallow and keep reading from my paper.

"My mom said that my great-great-grandparents were killed by the Nazis, but that Avraham escaped. He spoke seven different languages perfectly. He escaped by convincing people everywhere he went that he was one of them and not Jewish. And he kept one big diamond hidden in his butt cheeks.

"Just reporting the facts," I add.

"Understood," Rabbi Bob says.

A few of the kids chuckle, but not Gideon. "It's a

good hiding place," he says. His nose sounds stuffy, I'm guessing because of the bagel situation. "I think your great-grandfather was really smart."

"My mom said the only ticket he could get out of Europe was to Mexico. So that's where he went. When he got there, he took the diamond out of his butt cheeks and started a jewelry business."

"What a story," Rabbi Bob says.

"My mom visited him in Mexico every summer when she was growing up. He wore a big gold ring with a diamond on his pinky so he'd never forget what saved his life."

"I don't think it was the diamond that saved him," Gideon slowly calls out.

Everyone turns to face him.

"I think it was his brain." Gideon brushes the hair out of his eyes. "Yapa says, 'It's not what you have, it's how you use it.' I think Yapa is right."

"I think Yapa is right, too, Gideon," Rabbi Bob says.

"And it doesn't make sense, what Avery said, about the Nazis," Gideon adds.

Rabbi Bob tugs at his beard. "Can you say more about that, Gideon? Tell us what you're thinking." This is the first time I've ever heard a teacher actually want to hear *more* from Gideon. I'm kind of curious, too.

"It doesn't make sense what the Nazis thought, that the world would be better without Jews. Because Jewish people are just people. And all Jews are different. It's not fair to put us all together just because we have the same religion. Or to separate us from other people just because we don't."

Exactly, I'm thinking. I look at Gideon and, even though I've known him basically forever, it feels strangely like the first time I ever saw him.

"You're very wise, Gideon. Has anyone ever told you that before?"

Gideon nods. "Yapa."

Rabbi Bob looks at the rest of us. "What do you think about what Gideon is saying? Is it fair to lump a whole group of people together based on religion? Or race? Or gender?"

Without a chance to stop myself, I blurt out, "We're being lumped together right now in Hebrew school, just because we're Jewish." Even though it's true, I'm majorly wishing I kept my mouth shut. And now it's too late to take back. I look down and think, *Please, don't ask me to say more about what I just said. Please.*

"Interesting point, Avery. I'd like you to say more," Rabbi Bob says.

I try to swallow but my mouth feels like it's been stuffed with a wad of cotton balls. "I mean, my parents make me come to Hebrew school every year and I'm pretty sure it's just because I'm Jewish. And they love to give me speeches about famous Jewish people. They've told me about all the famous Jewish athletes, every Jewish person ever involved with making Star Wars, and about a gazillion famous Jewish scientists. It's like they think Jews are so much better than everyone else, and if I know about all the cool famous people who are Jewish I will suddenly love going to Hebrew school."

"Let me guess," Rabbi Bob says, "it didn't work."

"Well, I mean, all these famous Jewish people are amazing."

"Okay, so at least we can agree on that," Rabbi Bob says.

Everybody in the room is staring at me, which is one of my least favorite situations to be in. And still the words keep falling out of my mouth. "But they're amazing because they're amazing," I say, "Not because they're Jewish. I think Tom Brady is amazing, and he's not Jewish. I think George Lucas is amazing, and he's not Jewish. I think every astronaut who's ever lived in the International Space Station is amazing, and only two of them were Jewish. A lot of people who are not Jewish are amazing. And I'm sure a lot of people who *are* Jewish are *not* so amazing. Ask Morah Neetza about her ex-husband if you don't believe me."

My heart feels like it is going to thump out of my chest. This is the most I've ever said in Hebrew school in my whole life. So much for laying low and keeping under the radar. "It's like Gideon said. It's not okay for the Nazis to lump the Jews together for a bad reason, right? So why is it okay to lump the Jews together for a good reason? It's not like people have a choice what group they're born into. I didn't do anything to be Jewish. So why should I feel like I'm better than someone else just because my parents force me to go to Hebrew school?"

"Is that why you think they send you to Hebrew school? So that you feel special?" Rabbi Bob asks. All the kids' eyes are going back and forth between Rabbi Bob and me like they're watching a tennis match. Which I wish they were, because that would mean at least I was playing tennis.

"Honestly, I don't have a clue why they send me to Hebrew school," I admit. "None of the reasons they've told me so far make sense. Least of all the one about how I should be proud to be Jewish because Albert Einstein and Sandy Koufax were Jewish."

"Don't forget Rabbi Bob, too."

He's cracking jokes and I just want this to be over. Wasn't today supposed to be my first lightsaber training, anyway?

"You've stumped me with a very good question," Rabbi Bob says. "*Why do I have to go to Hebrew school?*" He sighs, and strokes his beard.

"Maybe Avery is asking, 'Why be Jewish?'" Gideon says.

Exactly, I'm thinking. What's the point.

Rabbi Bob looks at Gideon. "Maybe you're right," he says. He chuckles and adds, "I'm a rabbi, I should know this, right?"

"Probably," Gideon says.

"Yes, it is a good question," Rabbi Bob says to all of us. "Challenging, but good. And if there's one thing Jews have a history of appreciating—aside from a nice pastrami sandwich on rye—it's a good, challenging question with lots of possible answers that can be argued over for thousands of years."

Little Basha's big brown eyes widen. "You think we argued about this question for *thousands of years*? Like we even argued with the dinosaurs?"

"I certainly argued about it with my parents," Rabbi Bob says. "And they were definitely dinosaurs."

"How come you didn't want to go to Hebrew school, Rabbi Bob? Hebrew school is fun." Sweet, innocent Little Basha.

"Why in the world would I want to go to Hebrew school when I could be playing ball in the street instead? Or going up to the roof of our apartment and launching bottle rockets?"

"Exactly," I say.

"Hebrew school was the last place on earth I wanted to be. That's why my poor parents had to drag me there kicking and screaming every week."

"And they never told you why you had to go, either?" I ask. Just as Rabbi Bob is about to answer, a small group of grown-ups enter the back of the sanctuary.

"Welcome, come on in, we won't bite!" Rabbi Bob cheerfully waves to them. The group steps in closer with their notepads and fancy clothes. Rabbi Bob explains to us, "These nice folks are on the committee to find a permanent rabbi for you. With any luck, you'll be free of me and my *meshugas* in no time at all."

Little Basha in the front row raises her hand and calls out at the same time, "What's mushygotts?"

Rabbi Bob laughs and answers, "*Meshugas* is a Yiddish

term for nonsense, or foolishness. Someone with plenty of *meshugas* is *meshuggeneh*. My favorite way to be, quite frankly."

Little Basha cries out, "I'm mesugary, too!" The grown-ups in the back smile with their mouths, but their faces seem less convinced. They shuffle away.

"To answer your question, Avery," Rabbi Bob continues, "my parents most certainly told me why I had to go to Hebrew school." I scooch forward in my seat. "They told me, 'Either you get into that classroom or Papa will *shmits* your *tukkhes* until it looks like a piece of lox on a bagel.' It was a very motivating explanation."

"What's a *tukkhes*?" Little Basha asks.

Rabbi Bob points to his butt, which makes her giggle. Which makes the rest of us giggle.

This could very possibly be my first Hebrew school giggle. It feels strange. But not bad.

"Speaking of my *tukkhes*," he says, "your teachers are going to *shmits* mine if I don't get you to your classrooms ASAP." He waves his hands for us to go. "Alas, until we meet again!" he cries as we file out of the sanctuary.

Just before I reach the door, Rabbi Bob pulls me aside. "What a great discussion you started, Avery."

I shrug. He leans in.

"I haven't forgotten about our lightsaber training," he whispers. "I want you to know that. But I'm afraid we won't have time today. I have a replacement meeting with the committee now, so let's aim for next Tuesday, okay?"

I shrug again. "Whatever."

After all, when it comes to Hebrew school getting in the way of my dreams, I have lots of practice.

CHAPTER
12

Sunday Afternoon

"How was Hebrew school?" Mom asks on the way to football.

"Well, it didn't kill me, so I guess that's good," I tell her.

"Very good," she replies. "I'd hate to think of all that tuition going to waste."

For some reason, I keep hearing Gideon's voice in my head, and thinking about the stuff he said today. Which is weird. I usually try very hard not to think about Hebrew school. Too painful. But today, it felt ... different. Less like walking barefoot on shards of broken glass for three hours.

"Mom?" I ask. "You know Gideon, right?"

"Gideon Munk? Sure. Sweet kid. A little bit of a loose cannon and somewhat kooky, I guess, but sweet. Why?"

"No reason, really. It's just that, I don't know, I've known him a long time, but don't know anything about him. He had a lot to say in Hebrew school today."

"That's nice," Mom says. "Maybe you'll get to know him better this year." We pull up to the field. "Hop out and I'll park the car," she tells me. "And try not to get killed out there today. It would be a rather ironic tragedy to have survived Hebrew school only to get murdered by a bunch of ruffians on the football field, don't you think, sweetie?"

"Super-ironic."

I can see the Bears warming up at the far sideline. Gideon is doing some kind of weird burpee while breaking all the rules of personal space. Mom called him a loose cannon, but in a way, I think he's more like a mystery flavor. Can't quite figure him out.

That's kind of cool, actually. To be mysterious like that.

He comes plodding over as soon as he sees me. "Hey, Avery," he pants. "Ready for the game?"

"Sure." Gideon is doing a very strange version of high knee kicks beside me and I'm thinking it will be a miracle if he doesn't crack his own skull with his knee caps. It looks really funny. "Who taught you how to do those?" I say, laughing.

He starts laughing, too. "No one!" he says. "You should try it! It's very invigorating!"

"Nah, think I'll pass." By the time we get to the rest of the Bears, Gideon has tired himself out. But my face is still smiling. "Hey, Gideon?"

He looks up at me. His cheeks are bright red and sweat is dripping down the side of his face. The game hasn't even started and he looks totally cooked.

"I got a question for you."

He looks at me sideways. His nose is still wonky, for sure. *You should have stayed with Gideon when he got hurt.* The voice is clear in my head, and this time, it's not the little angel's voice. It's mine.

"Yeah?"

"You into Star Wars?" I ask.

Gideon honks out a laugh.

"Well, obviously," he tells me.

•

"NO ROOM FOR WEAKNESS!" a booming voice shouts from the stands.

When I follow the voice to its source, not surprisingly, I see Damon's dad. Brick-wall shoulders in a Bears hoodie, permanently angry eyebrows, deathly spiky faux hawk, holding up his phone to record the game, hollering like a football coach from The Dark Side. His voice is so loud it's practically vibrating my helmet. Seriously. Did anyone ever teach him about volume control?

Next to him is that weird old man from our first game, still puffing away on his cigar. This time he's wearing a white yachting cap with black and gold trim and a baggy tie-dyed t-shirt. I can see from the stink eye he's giving Damon's dad that he's annoyed, too.

Coach has us doing warm-ups on the side of the field. Gideon and I are throwing the football and I'm thinking maybe Mom's description of Gideon is pretty accurate. From the way he throws the ball, it really does seem like he's shooting off loose cannons. Maybe that's why he's keeping his helmet on. Across the field are the Browns. Everyone says they're the worst team in the league. So maybe we have a chance.

"NO PAIN NO GAIN, D!" Damon's dad yells like cracking thunder. "BE A WINNER, SON, YOU HEAR! SHOW 'EM WHO'S IN CHARGE!"

Seems a little dramatic for a bunch of kids suited up for a football game.

Damon's dad has left his seat in the stands and is walking over to us. I swear I can hear Darth Vader's Imperial March playing in the background. "Maybe he's hangry," Gideon says. "Sometimes I get angry when I'm hungry, too."

"Something tells me this guy's problem has nothing to do with hunger," I say quiet enough that Darth Damon's Dad can't hear me. He walks right up to Damon. "YOU GONNA BE A WINNER OR A LOSER, SON?" he barks.

No volume control. None.

Damon nods.

"LOUDER, SON!" Darth Damon's Dad shouts.

"Winner!" Damon says.

"THAT'S MY BOY! A WINNER! NO TIME FOR LOSERS AROUND HERE!"

Damon nods again. I watch as his dad marches back to the stands. He plunks down on the bleacher next to the old man, who is looking at me. For a moment, we make eye contact. He shrugs and tosses his hands in the air as if to say, "Don't worry about it." A puff of smoke clouds his face.

Gideon says, "I feel sorry for Damon," in his slow, gravelly voice. He awkwardly tips a cup of water into his mouth through his helmet, emptying the last of it.

"Sorry? For Damon? Why?" I know that Gideon is a little weird, but now I'm wondering if he's crazy. "In case you haven't noticed, that kid is pure evil. Have you seen your nose lately? And from the looks of it, his evilness might be genetic."

"Evilness isn't like eye color, Avery. You don't just inherit it."

"Well, even if he didn't inherit it, he's doing a great job keeping the tradition of evilness alive. It's a waste of time to feel sorry for him. Better just to stay as far away from him as you can. That's my plan, anyway."

Gideon shrugs off my suggestion, unconvinced. "I'm going for a refill." He wanders toward the water jug with his helmet bobbling on his shoulders.

As he fills his cup, he calls out to me with a huge smile on his face, "Hey, Avery! It's lemonade in here!" He starts walking slowly back toward me, taking tiny sips from his overflowing cup. Out of nowhere, Damon sneaks up behind him.

"Turn around, Gideon!" I cry. But it's too late.

Damon reaches under Gideon's loose helmet from the

back and lifts it off in one quick move. Gideon loses his balance and trips forward, sending the entire content of his cup flying in my direction.

Damon drops Gideon's helmet on the ground, laughing like an evil Sith would laugh if evil Siths laughed. "Loser!" he yells.

My jersey is dripping with sticky pink lemonade as Gideon gets back up to his feet. "Ready to reconsider feeling sorry for Damon yet?" I ask.

•

Fourth quarter, fourth down, and nine at the fifty-yard line, we're down by thirteen points.

Ethan, the wide receiver who is not me, has the ball. He gets tackled, hits the ground, and *then* releases the ball. A player from the Browns picks up the ball and starts running as if he has no idea about the rules of football—releasing the ball after getting tackled is a down, *not* a fumble. The thief runs the ball twenty yards before getting tackled, and the ref gives the Browns the ball! Totally and completely unfair. The ball should have been ours, 100%, no doubt about it.

"YOU GOTTA BE KIDDING ME!" Darth Damon's Dad shouts. "WHAT, ARE YOU BLIND, REF?!" he screams. "I GOT THE WHOLE THING ON VIDEO!"

Okay, I have to admit that I sort of agree with Darth Damon's Dad, who begins shouting a string of super-inappropriate four-letter words and even a few longer than four letters. Ref points at him and blows the whistle. "You! Out!" she yells.

"YOU GOTTA BE KIDDING ME! YOU TELLING ME *I* GOTTA GO? *I'M* NOT THE ONE WHO MADE THE LOUSY CALL! HOW ABOUT YOU GET YOUR EYES CHECKED, SWEETHEART? MAYBE THEN YOU CAN START BEING A *REAL* REF!"

Darth Damon's Dad glares at all of the parents sitting in the stands, which includes my parents, who look beyond horrified. "WHAT? *I'M* NOT THE ONE WHO MADE THE BAD CALL! I GOT THE PROOF RIGHT HERE!" He waves his phone around. "THIS IS WHAT HAPPENS WHEN YOU PUT IN A LADY REF! WHAT A JOKE!"

Ref is talking privately to Coach. Then they approach Damon's dad in the stands. I hear him say something about this being a free country and barking a few more inappropriate words that my mom would describe as "colorful." I look to my parents for a clue, but they look at me and shrug.

"YOU CAN'T KICK ME OUTTA THE GAME, CUZ I'M LEAVING!" Darth Damon's Dad shouts. "D!" he yells, "JUST REMEMBER, YOU'RE A WINNER!" From the dramatic way he storms off, he should be wearing a black cape.

We all turn to Damon, who's running in place and pounding his chest like an ape.

No, really. I once read about why apes pound their chest. It's a warning sign for younger apes to back off unless they want to get their butts kicked. That, or it's part of a victory cry, which this occasion is most definitely not.

I get put in for the end of the game, again. I guess Coach is still testing me out. He puts me in as free safety on defense. I run my hardest to block the deep throws but no matter how fast I run, the Browns are faster.

Damon takes down four players in the last ten minutes of the game, including Jaxon from our math class, who is the Browns' quarterback.

But we still lose, with plenty of help from Gideon, who accidentally backed into Sean, our quarterback, just as the ball was snapped to him.

When the ref calls the end of the game, Damon throws down his helmet and shouts "NOOOO!" There is a crack in his voice and he wipes his eyes with the back of his hand. Jaxon limps up to Damon and says, "Guess it's too late for you to quit now to save face," then limps away.

Damon shouts, "Shut up!" He runs off.

Gideon and I look at each other. "If I didn't know any better, I'd say that boy was crying," I say to Gideon.

Gideon's brows crinkle up into a worried expression. He trots off toward Damon but is intercepted by Rabbi Bob and his two dogs. I drop to my knees and pretend to be tying my shoelaces so that Rabbi Bob doesn't see me.

"*Shalom*, Gideon!" Rabbi Bob cries from the other side of the fence. "How was your game?" I discreetly take a peek to see the very big dog and the very small dog tugging at their leashes and Rabbi Bob struggling to keep them in place.

"Oh, hi, Rabbi Bob!" he replies. "Not our best game."

"Maybe next time," Rabbi Bob says. The dogs keep tugging. "I'd better be going. Boris and Natasha over here are ready to go home."

"See you soon, Rabbi Bob!" Gideon calls out. He begins to trot toward Damon again. My stomach knots up. With Rabbi Bob out of sight, it's safe for me to stand. Once he reaches him, Gideon taps Damon on the shoulder, which seems suicidal. Whatever Gideon said, Damon didn't like it. He gives Gideon a royal shove and he topples over. As soon as Damon is far enough, I go to Gideon, who is slowly pushing himself up to his feet.

"Do you have a death wish or something?" I ask. "What did you say to him?"

"I told him he played a good game."

"What?! Are you crazy? Why would you do that, Gideon? He's evil. Especially to you!"

"Yeah, but he *did* play a good game."

"That's like telling Darth Sidious he's got some cool tricks! Would you do that, too?"

Gideon thinks quietly for a moment. "If I thought it might help, I would."

We walk the rest of the way to the parking lot in silence. Because what am I supposed to say to that?

CHAPTER
13

Monday, Regular School

Today at school, I try something new.

I sit next to Gideon during lunch.

I've never done it before.

Usually, I spend lunch eating and working out plays in my notebook.

But not today. When I walk into the cafeteria and I see Gideon sitting by himself at a table, I just plop down next to him.

"I have something for you," I say.

"What?" Gideon asks.

I unzip my lunchbox and hand him a small glass vial plugged with a cork. "Potion #18," I say. "My best so far."

Gideon smiles and wipes his greasy hands on his shirt, then takes the vial. "Nice!" he says.

I kind of like Gideon's enthusiasm. He doesn't even know what Potion #18 is.

"Go ahead, open it," I say, "but be careful. You don't want to spill that stuff. It's super-powerful."

Gideon's eyes light up. He pops off the cork. The odor quickly escapes. It smells worse than a thousand of Champ's rotted dog farts. Gideon's eyes water and he starts to gag.

"Close it before anyone else gets a whiff," I whisper.

"That is amazing!" Gideon says with a huge smile. "I almost threw up! I never smelled anything so bad in my life!"

"I know. Told you it was my best."

"You made that?"

"Stinky potions. It's a hobby of mine."

Gideon is shaking the vial and holding it up to the light with a dreamy expression on his face. "What's in there?" he asks.

"I normally don't disclose that type of information," I say, "but I can trust you, right?"

Gideon nods in a way that makes me believe I can.

I lean in closer so no one else can hear. "Crushed ginkgo berries, moldy refried beans, and a small strip of a dirty sock that I accidentally left outside and my neighbor's cat peed on it." I nod proudly. "That was an amazing stroke of luck. Skittles must have been marking her territory on it." Gideon shakes the vial again. "Soaked it in a pH neutral solution overnight," I add. "You can keep it."

"Really?"

"Sure. I have another vial at home."

"Wow. Thanks, Avery. This is the second-best thing anyone has ever given me."

"I have to know what the first was."

"Yapa once gave me a giant piece of driftwood from Tahiti that looks *exactly* like Jabba the Hutt."

"Yapa?"

"Yep. He's my grandfather."

"Right. The Hungarian grandfather with the mouth of a drunken sailor."

"How did you know he was a sailor?"

"He was? Really? I thought my mom was just saying it, like an expression."

"He was a sailor his whole life."

"But there aren't any oceans around Hungary, are there?"

"Good point. I meant after he left Hungary."

"How old was he when he left?"

"Seventeen. He said it was a calling."

"To become a sailor?"

"Yep. He said he was born with a pirate's soul, and that not even a land-locked dump could stop him from a life on the sea."

"A grandfather pirate."

"My mom made him come back this past summer. She said Yapa was too old to be living on boats. She said it was time for him to return to civilization. Yapa says civilization isn't so civilized. He said he would rather die happy at sea than rot slowly on earth. But when my mom told him I was growing up very fast, and that he'd miss out on knowing his only grandchild if he stayed at sea much longer, then Yapa changed his mind. He says I'm worth more to him than all the oceans in the world. Which, coming from Yapa, means a lot."

How did I not know any of this?

"People think that Yapa is crazy, but according to Yapa, people are crazy."

Gideon peels off the bread of his tuna sandwich, adds a layer of chips and bright green peppers, puts it back together, and eats the whole thing in three bites. "You've probably seen him at our games. Funny hats. Smokes cigars," he says with a stuffed mouth. "We're best friends."

"So that's Yapa."

"My mom fixed up a room for him in our house, but he prefers to bunk with me. Says it feels more like how sailors are supposed to sleep, stacked up and talking late into the night."

The bell rings. Lunch went faster than usual today. Too fast.

"Thanks again for Potion #18," Gideon says holding up the vial.

"Use it wisely," I say in a deep, serious voice.

"Will do!" Gideon says cheerfully, giving me a thumbs-up with the hand holding the vial. This was not the best idea.

The vial slips from his hand. My stomach instantly drops to my feet in fear. Oh, no. How in the world am I going to explain the stench to the lunch ladies?

Luckily, I won't need to. Gideon drops to his knees and,

miraculously, catches it just before it hits the floor. The slick move reminds me of Super Bowl LI when Julian Edelman made the most epic catch in football history, half an inch before the ball hit the ground.

"Nice Edelman!" I say. And I mean it.

Gideon looks up and gives me a thumbs-up, this time with his other hand.

"Hey," he says as he's getting back to his feet, "want to come over to my house after football practice tomorrow? My mom has to work so Yapa is in charge. He's making goulash for dinner."

I have no idea what goulash is. But if Yapa's in charge and that's what he's making, I'm in.

"Goulash," I say, "sounds good."

CHAPTER
14

Tuesday Afternoon

"Sorry to interrupt, Morah Neetza," Rabbi Bob says a few minutes before the end of class. "But I need Avery for a little project we're working on."

Morah Neetza frowns. "Zis is 'ow it is around 'ere, I see," she scolds. "You want to take 'im, take!" she snaps.

Rabbi Bob actually looks a little afraid of Morah Neetza. "*Todah raba*, Morah Neetza. Thank you. Won't happen again, I promise." Rabbi Bob smiles nervously.

"Zis is what zey all say," I hear Morah Neetza complain as Rabbi Bob leads me out of the classroom.

Getting out early seriously feels like a jail break. I have no idea what Morah Neetza was teaching us because how am I supposed to pay attention to Morah Neetza when I know a real lightsaber exists and it's right down the hall in Rabbi Bob's office?

When we get to his office, I basically forget I'm even in a

synagogue because who ever heard of a synagogue that has *original Star Wars posters* hanging in the rabbi's office? Like the kind printed forever ago, in 1977.

"I didn't even know they still existed," I say, stepping up to get a closer look at the one with Luke and Leia in white costumes and a huge Darth Vader head looming in the background. He also has an autographed picture of Princess Leia on the wall.

"My first true love," he explains.

Yuck, I'm thinking. I'm totally *not* into true love.

I look around. I am in awe. Rabbi Bob's office is basically a Star Wars museum. Totally coo-coo-banana-split.

There are rows of shelves completely covered in Star Wars memorabilia, including the following: two ancient Star Wars lunchboxes, a model of the Millennium Falcon, about a million Star Wars action figures—regular and Lego, stormtrooper and Wookie Pez candy dispensers, tons of Star Wars books, a Darth Vader pencil holder, a Yoda coffee mug, and an R2-D2 pencil sharpener. And on the corner of his desk, a photo of his very huge and very small dogs wearing Princess Leia and Yoda costumes.

Seeing all this stuff gives me a mixed-up feeling. It's majorly impressive, but I know it's all going to disappear soon. My voice cracks when I ask, "How come you have all this stuff here, if you're only temporary?"

Rabbi Bob offers me a purple Pez. "Maybe you should ask my wife. She very conveniently packed it all up for me as soon as she heard I'd have an office here. Something about it not fitting in our condo anymore and that maybe the kids at Hebrew school would enjoy it."

I finish the Pez, wishing the sugary crunch would last longer as I eye each item in his collection more carefully. And then I see it, propped on a special stand made to hold it upright.

The lightsaber.

Suddenly, nothing else in the room exists but me and the lightsaber.

Rabbi Bob chuckles. "If I didn't know any better, I'd think you were Moses at the burning bush." He gives me a little nudge toward the lightsaber. "Go ahead, you can touch it."

I look around the room. Nothing here to indicate that Rabbi Bob is an evil Sith mastermind.

Other than the fact that I know his lightsaber is red.

Here's the thing: When it comes to lightsabers, red is evil. To make my point, here is a sample list of Star Wars characters who use red lightsabers:

Count Dooku—evil.

Darth Maul—evil.

Darth Vader—evil. (Except in the end when he battles Emperor Palpatine to save his son's life. People never give him enough credit for that.)

Kylo Ren—evil.

Emperor Palpatine—crazy evil.

Rabbi Bob?

I look at Rabbi Bob. He's smiling at me. Not an I'm-smiling-because-I'm-about-to-kill-you-with-my-red-lightsaber kind of way. Just a regular little smile.

I look at the lightsaber.

It's just sitting there, looking amazing.

I decide it will be okay to give it a try.

I walk up slowly to the lightsaber. It looks so real. Nothing like the one I got for my seventh birthday, which is cool, but made out of flimsy plastic.

I lift it carefully from its stand.

It's so heavy I need two hands to hold it.

I raise it up and look carefully at the black and silver metal hilt, which is the part you hold. It contains a blade emitter shroud that holds the lens that converts the lightsaber's energy beam into a blade of super-hot plasma. I can only imagine the kyber crystal inside that powers the whole thing. Naturally occurring red kyber crystals are extremely rare, but maybe this one is artificially synthesized. Which would make Rabbi Bob so evil.

I try not to think about it.

"How do you turn it on?" I ask nervously.

"You must use The Force within yourself," Rabbi Bob replies in a slow, serious voice. "Close your eyes and repeat after me," he says, and then sings a prayer I've heard a million times before. "*Shema Y'Israel Adonai Elohaynu, Adonai Echad. Hear, O Israel, the Lord is God, the Lord is One.*" He adds, "The Shema is the single most important prayer in Judaism. It reminds us of The Force that binds us all together, that everything in the galaxy is one."

I take a deep breath and scrunch my eyes closed.

I repeat the Shema.

Nothing happens.

Rabbi Bob taps me on the shoulder. "And there's a little button on the left," he points out.

I'm afraid that I'll drop the lightsaber if I release my grip, so I slide my hand over to the button without letting go.

I press the button.

A deep zapping noise hums to life. The power from the glowing red light that suddenly beams from the handle nearly knocks me over, but I catch myself before it does. I widen my feet to a football stance. It feels like this thing weighs a thousand pounds with the energy of a rocket blasting from a launch pad.

"The Shema had nothing to do with turning this on, did it?" I ask, holding the lightsaber with a total death grip. I'm pretty sure if I drop it the beam will slice off my feet.

"Not a thing."

"Are you using the lightsaber as a trick to get me to believe in God?" My knuckles are completely white from my insanely tight grip, but I haven't sliced off my feet yet. So that's good. "Because if it is, it will never work. I'm a man of science. And besides," I add, "if you *were* using the lightsaber as a trick to get me to believe in God, you should have at least used a blue or green lightsaber. Red is a little creepy."

"Definitely not," Rabbi Bob laughs easily. "Whether or not you choose to believe in God is none of my business."

"But you're a rabbi. Isn't it your job to make people believe in God?"

"Is that what you think my job is?" he asks.

I nod. "Remember, when you said that? All that stuff about The Force being God, and it's your big job to teach us how to see it and use it."

Rabbi Bob strokes his beard and looks at me very quietly, almost like I'm a new kind of creature he's never seen before.

The lightsaber is getting heavier by the minute. The muscles in my arms are burning.

Finally, he says, "You're right, Avery. I did say that. And maybe part of my job is to help people connect with God. But ..."

Rabbi Bob looks at me again with that funny quiet stare.

"But what?" I ask. In my head, I remind myself not to drop the thousand-pound lightsaber and slice off my feet.

"But it has to be more than that. Hebrew school must have a purpose for a man of science like yourself besides forcing you to believe something you don't. Agree?"

I shrug and focus my attention on the lightsaber, which seriously feels like it's going to snap my arms in half. I try to straighten my elbows a little, but even that is super-hard. They make it look so easy in the movies.

"Good, now can you raise it up, like this?" Rabbi Bob

demonstrates with a baseball bat that he grabbed from the closet. I'm relieved he's not talking about God anymore.

The muscles in my arms are shaking like crazy. I've never lifted anything so heavy in my life. As I slowly raise the lightsaber, the deep zapping noise changes, just like in Star Wars. By the time I get it over my head, I'm getting sweaty and huffing and puffing as if I've just made a 100-yard touchdown.

"I am a Jedi, like my father before me," I whisper, pretending to be Luke from *Return of the Jedi*.

"Very good, Avery," Rabbi Bob tells me. "Now, let me help you lower it. I think raising it once over your head is enough for your first day. A fine start."

Rabbi Bob lowers the lightsaber with me, then takes it from my hands.

I cannot stop staring at the lightsaber. It is unspeakably amazing. I want very badly to hold it again, but Rabbi Bob puts it back on the stand.

"I don't mean to be rude, Rabbi Bob, but …" I swallow my disappointment, "… is that it for today? Just one teensy lift?"

"May I remind you that before today you'd never even rested a little pinky on a real lightsaber? Have you ever heard the expression *Give a man a finger and he takes the whole hand*?"

"Surprisingly, I have."

"One does not become a Jedi master overnight. One must show discipline, patience, and hard work."

"But the lightsaber is red and Jedi never use red lightsabers."

Rabbi Bob looks at me carefully. He is silent for too long. I'm starting to wonder if I should run for my life when he suddenly speaks to me in Yoda's voice.

"See things as black or white you must not," he says.

I'm confused. Weren't we just talking about the color red?

"Many shades of gray in between there are," he says, still in Yoda's voice.

Now he's talking about gray? "I don't understand."

There's a knock on the door. It creaks open and Mom pops her head in. "Sorry to interrupt, Rabbi Bob. I was just looking for Avery," she says, and then to me adds, "I came a little early, like you asked. I know you don't want to be late for football practice."

"Hello, Mrs. Green. Nice to see you," Rabbi Bob says. "I must say, what a son you have here. Very inquisitive mind. Unafraid to ask tough questions."

"I'll say," Mom replies. She looks at me and crosses her arms. "Did his questions get him in trouble today, Rabbi? Is that why he's in your office?"

Rabbi Bob laughs. "Questions are good, Mrs. Green, very good. And no, Avery's not in trouble at all. In fact, we've just begun our lightsaber training."

I'm sorry, did Rabbi Bob just tell my mom about our top-secret lightsaber training? Forget fainting. This time I think I'm going to actually die from shock.

Mom laughs. "Ah, a fellow Star Wars fanatic, I see. Well—" she checks her watch— "unless you want to skip football, Avery, it'll have to wait."

I can't believe it. Rabbi Bob told Mom the truth and she thought it was a joke. Either this guy is totally coo-coo-banana-split or a complete genius.

Or, an evil Sith mastermind.

It seems Mom has noticed that I haven't moved. "Get your things together and meet me in the car, chop, chop!" she instructs.

"So, you're out there, too," Rabbi Bob says after Mom leaves. "I've seen Gideon on the field, but I didn't know you played, as well. Same team?"

I look down and nod.

"Funny how I've missed you. I always see Gideon. I like to walk my dogs around the field after Hebrew school— maybe you've seen us?"

I look down and shake my head even though I've seen him plenty.

"Next time I'm out there I'll make sure to stop by and say hello. Maybe I'll even stay for next Sunday's game."

Please don't, I'm thinking. Getting used to Gideon on the team has been enough of a nut in my chocolate-chip cookie. Two nuts might be too much.

CHAPTER
15

Tuesday Afternoon, Football Practice

I'm not sure how long I can wait until I get to use the lightsaber again. Like for real, not just lifting it up and putting it back down. I mean, that was okay, but I would hardly call it Jedi training.

Real Jedi training would be way more cool than that. I would need to be placed in a clan and taught political strategy, galactic law, language, and the sciences—yes, please, and thank you very much! I'd be taught the ways of The Force and all the proper forms of lightsaber combat. I'd have my own training lightsaber until I was sent to the caves of Ilum where I would find my kyber crystal and craft my own. There would be grueling graduation tests. I would be paired with a Master for one-on-one training.

See what I mean?

So this business of picking up the lightsaber and putting it back down seems a little rinky-dink, if you ask me.

"You seem quiet, Avery," Mom says on our way to football practice, interrupting my visions of traveling through space with my Master on a Council-appointed Jedi training mission. "What are you thinking about?"

"Nothing," I say, because I don't think she understands Council-appointed Jedi missions, and I don't have it in me to explain it again right now.

"Excited about football practice?" she asks.

"I guess."

We pull into the parking lot. She turns to me and raises her eyebrows. "You guess?"

"I was just thinking about the stuff me and Rabbi Bob were working on," I tell her as I scan the field. No sign of Rabbi Bob and his dogs spying on me yet. Just a bunch of players running laps. I see Damon at the head of the pack. "But I'm ready for practice. It'll be good. We need it. Our first two games didn't go very well."

"Chin up, kid. I'll pick you up at Gideon's house after practice," she reminds me as I get out of the car.

I jog over to the field and Gideon sprints in his ploddy Gideon way to catch up to me.

"Hey, Avery," he says, out of breath, smiling.

As usual, Damon comes up from behind, about to lap us. "Oh, look," he says, "it's *gill weed* and his little friend."

"Hey, Damon," Gideon says with a friendly wave, like nothing between them has happened.

"If I were you, *gill weed*, I'd keep your distance," he spits out, which makes zero sense. *He's* the one who came up to *us.* "You're lucky I don't smash your face in for stinking so bad at football. If it weren't for you, we might actually have a chance of winning," he sneers and races ahead.

"Seriously, Gideon, why are you nice to that guy?" I whisper as we circle up with the team.

"Because I get the feeling no one else is," he whispers back.

•

Gideon lives close to the field. After a five-minute walk, he stops and says, "Here we are," and I stop and think, *Whoa, not like the others.* This is because Gideon's house does not look like any of the other houses on his street. Or any street. For one thing, the entire garage door is painted to look like a jungle. And I don't mean like a little kid's version of a jungle made from washable paint. I mean a jungle, like with jungle trees and jungle birds and a huge jaguar with piercing green eyes looking like it's about to walk straight out of it and possibly eat us alive.

"That's some garage door you got there," I say.

Gideon says, "Mom likes to paint."

The pathway leading to his house is lined with colorful lanterns and there are chickens pecking around the grass in the front yard. As we get closer to the front door, I hear a funny sound, like a tinny cry.

"Goats," is all Gideon says, as if that should explain everything.

As soon as we open the door, Yapa's deep gravelly voice calls out to us. "In the kitchen!" he shouts.

Gideon waves me in. "This way," he says, and walks me past about a thousand very ancient-looking wooden masks hanging on the walls. "Yapa collected all of those from around the world," he explains as I slow down to look at them. Some have carved mouths with vicious teeth, others are brightly painted, some have crazy hair sticking out on top. "Every time he found one he liked, he'd mail it to me. This one is my favorite," he says pointing to a mask covered in black swirls with big disk-shaped eyes and a tongue sticking out.

In the kitchen, Yapa is standing over a big, steaming pot on the stove with a puffy white chef's hat tilted on his head. A slobbery, unlit cigar is dangling from his lips. He turns toward us with one hand on his hip and the other stirring with a tall wooden spoon. His glasses are fogged from the steam and he's wearing an apron that looks like a lady in a red polka dot bikini from the neck down.

"Practice okay?" Yapa asks. The cigar bobbles when he talks. He hands us a bowl filled with tiny green balls. "You need a nosh?"

Gideon takes a handful and pops them in his mouth. "Not our best," he says. "No one wants to be a Bear because Bears don't win." Green crumbs fly from his mouth as he talks.

I don't know what he's eating, but out of politeness I take one and bite into it. My mouth suddenly feels like it's on fire. I start coughing and my eyes tear up. "Wow," I say once the tiny green fireball has gone down my throat. "What is that?"

Yapa's cigar bobbles harder as he laughs. "Dried wasabi peas," he says, "good for ya!" He takes a big handful and drops it in his mouth. "Puts hair on your chest!"

Gideon smiles at Yapa. He turns to me, shaking his head. "They don't really," he whispers.

"You gotta know this about Yapa," says Yapa, "half the time I tell the 100% truth." He leans over the pot and takes a deep inhale. Puffs of steam cloud over his face. He turns back to us with his glasses all fogged up. "Question is, which half?"

Gideon pats Yapa on the back. "Anyone ever tell you that you're nuts, Yapa?"

"Every day of my life!" He puts his arm around Gideon's shoulder. "How about we eat, boys? Goulash is ready and perfect." There are bowls set for each of us and a basket of rolls in the middle of the table.

After we sit down, Yapa says, "So what's this nonsense about Bears never winning?" He scoops an enormous spoonful of saucy noodles with chunks of meat into his mouth.

"It's true," I say. "We lost both games so far. And we're up against the Cowboys next week. They won both of their games *and* they were last year's league champions."

Gideon reaches across the table for a roll.

"Bah! Two games?" Yapa cries, startling Gideon, who

knocks into my bowl of goulash. Of course, it lands right in my lap.

Yapa is laughing hard with a full mouth as he howls, "Would you look at these two—*Shlemiel* and *Shlimazel*! Ha! I love it! Made for each other, boys!" He shovels in another chunky spoonful. I'm digging out goulash by the fistful as Yapa continues, "Two games is peanuts! You want to hear a story about *real* losing?"

Gideon and I nod.

"So this was in, let me think, '82, I believe. Long haul. Oil tanker. Somewhere in the Pacific, ya couldn't pay me to remember exactly. Hadn't seen land for weeks. Crew gettin' itchy, ready to get back to their wives, their girlfriends, their wives *and* their girlfriends, et cetera, et cetera. A few of us was in the galley. Poker—that was our game. See, that's what we did when we had downtime out at sea. We played cards, we drank, we told stories. That's what we did. None of them smart phones to keep us stupid, you know what I mean?"

I don't exactly know what he means, but I definitely want to hear more.

"Cookie was drunk as a skunk under the table—forget him. I was down by a couple hundred bucks, and Tiny wants to keep playing." Yapa peers over the rim of his thick black glasses. "You with me?"

Gideon and I nod.

"Now, when Tiny wants to keep playing, all's you can do is keep playing."

"Tiny?" I ask.

"Picture a 300-pound Russian pit bull that learned how to walk upright and grunt a few syllables. That's Tiny," Yapa explains.

Gideon and I nod.

"'But Tiny,' I says, 'I'm outta cash. You cleaned me out. How do you expect me to go another round?' 'Your shoes,' he says, and points to my shoes. Now I don't know what Tiny wants with my shoes, but if Tiny wants to play for my shoes, Tiny is going to play for my shoes. We play another round, me and Tiny, and I lose. I start to pack up the cards and the chips, but Tiny wants more. 'Your socks,' he grunts."

Yapa peers over his glasses. "Next he says, 'Your shirt.'" Yapa raises his eyebrows. "You see where this is going?"

Gideon and I nod.

"So this goes on until three in the morning and I'm down to my skivvies. Tiny starts laughing like you never seen a guy laugh. Face red like a beet, howling and shaking with laughter. Like he's gonna die from laughing. He scoops up my pile of clothes and walks outta the room like he just seen the best comedy show in town, and me, all's I have left to my name is a stinkin' pair of underwear and a story to tell you boys about how it is to lose."

I'm kind of stunned because no one ever told me a story like that. It had nothing at all to do with football, but somehow I feel less bad about being on a losing team. Gideon says, "That's a good one, Yapa, I liked that one," like he's heard a million.

"So how did you get your clothes back?" I ask.

Yapa laughs and laughs. "I didn't!" he howls. When he finally catches his breath he leans back in his chair and says, "You can't win 'em all, boys." He chews on his cigar. Then he leans forward and looks at us over the top of his glasses. "But some, you can. Don't give up. That's all. You want something, you keep at it."

I decide that this is the half that is 100% true.

CHAPTER
16

Sunday Morning

"Well, my young Padawans, I have good news and I have bad news," Rabbi Bob says at the start of Hebrew school. "The good news is that the synagogue has found a stellar candidate to become your full-time, permanent rabbi."

I suddenly get a weird feeling in my stomach, like the time I came home from school and Champ wasn't there to greet me at the door like she usually is. Turned out she got herself trapped in the pantry, but it took me a scary hour to find her and when I did, she was barfing up a combination of cheez doodles, beef jerky, and Oreos all over the floor. I was so relieved to find her that I wasn't even mad. That's how it is with me and Champ.

Anyway, when Rabbi Bob said "good news" I was expecting something, well, good. This makes me nervous for the bad news.

"And the bad news," he continues, "is that I need to

leave in a few minutes for one final meeting with the new rabbi. So, we won't have time for our next victim to go in the hot seat and share the story of her name. Basha—" he leans toward Little Basha in the front row— "you'll have your turn next time, okay?"

Little Basha shoves the crumpled piece of paper she'd been holding into her pocket and pouts while nodding her head slowly. Is she actually disappointed?

Because really, it's me who should be disappointed.

For one thing, if Rabbi Bob splits and it turns out I'm the only chump who had to do the whole name thing in the hot seat, that would be wildly unfair. Especially after I did such a good job.

I knew I shouldn't have done such a good job.

Second—and more importantly—this means no lightsaber training ... again!

I know Jedis are supposed to have an unnatural amount of discipline and patience and all that, but seriously, how long am I supposed to wait? Rabbi Bob has been promising me lightsaber training for just about forever at this point, and still the only thing he's let me do is one measly lift over my head. And now he's leaving!

"All right, kids." Rabbi Bob looks at his watch. "Time to head to your classrooms and I'll see you next week."

Little Basha from the front row hops up to the *bimah* and gives Rabbi Bob a hug. "You're funny," she says, squeezing him. I'm thinking, *What a waste.*

"Hey, Avery," Gideon says to me on the way to Morah

Neetza's room, "Thanks again for Potion #18. I've been testing it out in various locations."

"Nice," I say very unenthusiastically. I'm still mad about Rabbi Bob ditching my lightsaber training. And he didn't even say sorry.

"That stuff is like a force field," Gideon says. "One drop and no one wants to come near."

"Cool," I mutter.

Morah Neetza starts class saying things in Hebrew, but honestly all I can hear is blah, blah, blah. I have transferred all of my mental energy to our big game against the Cowboys this afternoon.

CHAPTER
17

Sunday Afternoon

On my way to the game I try to shake off the sitting disease I got in Hebrew school. As soon as I get out of the car, I drop and do ten burpees. The blood starts to flow in my body again. I vanquish sitting disease.

I remember Yapa's words. "Don't give up. You want something, you keep at it." I repeat this in my head as I cross the field.

But the truth is, we're going to need a lot more than a few words from a weird old pirate to beat the reigning champs.

I see the Cowboys huddled around their coach. I've heard rumors that the Cowboys' coach has a habit of putting in older kids and lying about their ages so the team can have a size advantage. But I don't believe in rumors.

I believe in science.

I slow down as I jog past the Cowboys.

And scientific observation is telling me that they are way, way bigger than us.

I make my way to the Bears. Coach is reviewing opening plays in a huddle. I notice a few players are missing.

"Avery, good, you're here," he says. This surprises me. I was under the impression that Coach hadn't yet noticed that I existed.

"We're down a couple of players today, but I like your focus on the field," he says. Which surprises me even more. I mean, I do have excellent focus on the field, but I didn't know that he thought so, too. Guess he was paying attention to me at practice, after all.

Or he's desperate.

"Keep to your routes and give me some fast feet. You got that?" he says.

I'm not sure I'm hearing correctly. Because it sounds like Coach is putting me in to start. My stomach does a backflip and I suddenly feel very queasy.

"I want you in position when Sean's pass gets to you," Coach adds.

I have to give him a thumbs-up because my tongue is working very hard to suppress the wave of barf creeping up the back of my throat. I can't believe I'm starting.

Sean is the quarterback. Strong arm, not consistent with aim. But I can definitely work with it.

Coach goes through the rest of the offensive starting players, making sure we're all on the same page. We put our hands in the middle and chant *Go, Bears!* but it sounds a little pathetic with so few players. We scatter into our positions. Only Gideon is left on the bench for backup.

I look out into the stands and see my parents wrapped in their fleece sweatshirts, hugging their mugs of coffee. They clap as soon as they see me, which is kind of embarrassing and kind of nice.

The Cowboys get lined up on defense.

Up close, they look even bigger.

Ref blows the starting whistle.

The center snaps the ball back to Sean.

And we're off.

•

Off to a decent start!

We score our first touchdown before the first quarter is up! Incredible! The Cowboys tie it up quickly, but then we pull ahead with a second touchdown midway through the second quarter! Double incredible! Coach is pleased.

"Keep it up, boys!" he tells us as we fuel up on Gatorade and orange slices.

Mom and Dad look happy even though I haven't scored. They're probably just happy that I haven't gotten a concussion yet, which counts as way more than a touchdown in their world.

A galaxy away from Darth Damon's Dad's world, where winning is everything.

"GET IN THERE, D!" he shouts from the stands at the start of the second half. "TAKE WHAT'S YOURS,

SON!" Even in the middle of play, his voice sends shivers down my spine.

But it seems to work on Damon because not a minute after his dad's booming command, Damon shoves our cornerback out of the way to make a killer interception and runs the ball forty yards before the Cowboys' offensive lineman tackles him. Damon leaps to his feet, yelling, "YEAH! YEAH! WHO'S THE MAN?!"

Damon's smug expression makes me want to punch him in the face but I refrain, because it really was a killer interception. And because punching him would mean certain death for me. Gideon jogs up to Damon from the bench to give him a high five, but Damon ignores him.

Coach calls a quick time out to review our plays now that we've got the ball back.

We get ourselves into position. I can still hear Damon's voice bragging, "WHO'S THE MAN! WHO'S THE MAN!" The clock starts.

The center hikes the ball back to Sean. I run fast and deep into the corner. I'm exactly in position when out of nowhere comes Damon trying to catch Sean's pass—the one meant for me. He misses, obviously, and in the process gets me off course so that when the pass lands, it hits the ground with a loud, dejected thud.

And a big Cowboys linebacker crashes sideways into me, sending *me* to the ground with a loud, dejected thud.

I feel the pain of good times ending.

I feel the pain of the Cowboys suddenly remembering they are the reigning champs.

I feel the pain of evil Damon being too stupid to know where his zone ends and I feel the pain of his greediness keeping anyone else from having a crack at the ball.

Because I had it! I'm 100% positive I had it.

Coach calls another time out.

My parents rush to the bench in an overly dramatic fashion and frantically wave different numbers of fingers in front of me. "How many fingers am I holding up?" they ask simultaneously.

"Seriously, guys?"

"Just answer us!"

Mom is rifling through her purse and pulls out her phone with the flashlight on. "Look into the light!" she says nervously. "Now blink!"

"I didn't even hit my head."

"Are his pupils dilating properly?" Mom asks Dad. "I can't tell! Blink again, Avery!"

"Who's the president, Avery?" Dad blurts. "When's your birthday? What's your favorite flavor of ice cream?"

"Jelly Bean Dream. And I'm fine. Really. Except for the fact that you're going to make me blind with that light in my face."

My parents insist that I sit out the rest of the game. Coach takes their side. Which means Gideon, the only backup we have, takes my place on the field.

Can the game get any worse? I'm afraid to ask.

From the bench I have to witness a string of embarrassing fumbles, two humiliating interceptions, and passes from Sean that are so off I'm starting to wonder if his elbow is screwed on backwards. We've gone from having a clear lead to a tie and time is running out.

It's so nerve-wracking that even Darth Damon's Dad has quit hostilely coaching from the sidelines and is just pacing a ditch into the grass.

Coach buries his face in his hands.

With nineteen seconds left in the game, there is only one move left for us to make. And Sean knows it.

The Hail Mary.

This crazy long pass is only ever made in total desperation, with very little chance of success. But we have nothing to lose.

He goes for it.

Damon races down the sideline to catch the ball, and just as it seems like he might make it, Gideon, who is trying to block a Cowboy, trips and rolls directly into Damon's path. Damon runs right over him and lands on his face.

As if this isn't bad enough.

The Cowboys' safety is right there to pick the ball at the thirty-yard line. He hooks around and runs like his butt is on fire and—I am completely not joking—scores a touchdown for a pick six just as the ref blows the whistle to mark the end of the game.

Coach takes a walk down the sideline away from us, like

he's trying to pull himself together before he has to shake hands with the Cowboys' coach and the ref.

"YOU FREAK!" Damon shouts at Gideon, who is still on the ground. "LOSER!"

A ball wads up in my throat and my face becomes hot. I know I'm supposed to intervene somehow, to stop Damon from hurting my …

… from hurting Gideon. But … Gideon did screw up. My legs don't move. I want to help but I'm … I'm stuck.

"*Shalom*, Avraham!" a voice calls from behind. I turn around and see Rabbi Bob and his dogs. "No! Not Avraham! Whoops, sorry, Avery! I meant *shalom*, Avery!" I have the sudden urge to crawl into a deep hole. Rabbi Bob is behind the fence, opposite where Gideon and Damon went down, so I'm pretty sure he missed the whole thing. And I'm seriously hoping no one heard him calling me Avraham. He's waving at me with a dumb smile on his face as the two dogs yank on the leash. "Good to see you! Good luck with the game! Gotta run!" Thankfully, the very huge dog and the very small dog quickly pull him away.

"WHY DO YOU HAVE TO BE SUCH A SORRY EXCUSE?! IT'S YOUR FAULT WE LOST THIS GAME!" Damon screams. Gideon is now sitting up, cross-legged on the grass, while Damon hovers over him. Gideon is covering his ears.

From the stands, I see Yapa limping up to them. He's smoking a cigar.

"One more word outta you, ya little pissant," he says in a deep, gravelly voice, "and I will smear your face so firmly against a rock *and* a hard place that you'll have trouble remembering where your features ever used to be."

Everyone, including Damon, looks at Yapa, who is leaning against his carved wooden cane. The cigar is dangling from his wet, floppy lips. He is wearing a rainbow Sherpa hat with ear flaps and a pom-pom dangling to the side. The sleeves of his tattered sweatshirt are pushed up, showing a faded tattoo of a mermaid on one arm. The front of his sweatshirt has the words *Tecati My Body* on it.

I suddenly need to know what *Tecati My Body* means.

"Why don't you mind your own business, old man," Damon sneers.

Yapa peers long and slow over his big, black frames at Damon. "I took a dump this morning bigger than you," he finally says. He reaches his bony wrinkled hand toward Gideon. "Up you go, my boy," he says in a surprisingly gentle voice.

"Thanks, Yapa," Gideon replies.

Yapa takes the soggy cigar from his lips and kisses Gideon on the forehead. "You are smart to cover your ears," he crackles. "There was nothing he said that you need to hear."

"This is the one I was telling you about," Gideon says as they begin to walk away.

Yapa turns to watch Damon meet his father, who screams, "THIS TEAM IS A JOKE!" right in front of everybody.

"IF I WERE COACH, I'D BAG HALF THE PLAYERS! SEND THEM BACK TO FLAG FOOTBALL!" His eyes are bulging and his throat is puffed out like a frog. It looks like he's going to explode.

"I see what you mean," Yapa sighs. "His father is a buffoon."

"Maybe you shouldn't have been so hard on him, Yapa."

Yapa shrugs. "Ech," he says, "I done worse."

That night, I spend an extra-long time in my lab.

CHAPTER

18

Monday, Regular School

Gideon and I are tossing the football at recess. Or, rather, Gideon is tossing the ball and I'm running around like a confused squirrel trying to catch it, then I toss the ball and it goes right through the hole in his arms. "Sorry!" he says.

I feel slightly weird hanging out with Gideon at recess. It's the whole teachers and grocery stores, nuts and chocolate-chip cookies, Hebrew school and everything else.

But he asked and I said sure.

I'll admit, even though he can't throw or catch a ball to save his life, it's not so bad. Gideon is easy to talk to.

"Could morale for the Bears get any lower?" I say, tossing him the ball. "Like, if you had to locate our team's morale on Planet Earth, we'd be at the Dead Sea. Lowest point on dry land."

The ball slips untouched through his arms.

I add, "Thank you, Hebrew school, for teaching me one useful bit of information."

"Maybe the Marianas Trench," Gideon says, tossing the ball back to me. I have to run halfway across the playground to catch it. "Deepest part of all the oceans," he explains.

"Exactly," I say, out of breath. "Our morale would be in the Marianas Trench." I throw the ball back.

"Challenger Deep," he says, bending over to pick up the ball.

"Challenger Deep?" I race to make the catch. I toss.

"Challenger Deep," he repeats. The ball bounces off his stomach and drops to the ground. "Deepest point in the Marianas Trench."

"Challenger Deep," I agree.

This losing streak is eating us alive.

CHAPTER

19

Tuesday Afternoon

It's never going to happen. This whole thing is a lie. A tease. A cruel mirage.

Rabbi Bob is just stringing me along with promises of teaching me how to maneuver a real lightsaber. It's clear to me now that he has no intention of fulfilling his promise. He's not a Jedi Master. He is a liar who's not even going to be our rabbi anymore, so what difference does it make?

I show up at Hebrew school today, like I do every Tuesday afternoon, even though I don't want to, and what do I discover?

Nothing.

I discover nothing is happening.

Nothing except for Shemini Atzeret, that is.

"Didn't you get an email notification or something?" I ask Mom as we stand at the closed door to the synagogue reading the posted sign.

IN OBSERVANCE OF SHEMINI ATZERET
AND SIMCHAT TORAH,
THERE WILL BE NO HEBREW SCHOOL
TODAY.
PLEASE JOIN US WEDNESDAY EVENING
FOR A RAUCOUS CELEBRATION!

"Must have gotten lost in my inbox," she says while casually chomping on an apple. The wind starts to pick up and she zips up her coat. I pull on my hood. "Didn't Morah Neetza mention there was no school today last Sunday?" She takes another huge bite and chomps some more.

I find this chomping extremely annoying under the circumstances. Like she's not even bothered that we came all the way to Hebrew school only to find out there is no Hebrew school. Like she's not even sorry that she didn't look more carefully through her inbox. Like she's perfectly fine blaming me.

"Maybe," I say, stuffing my hands in my pocket. And that's the truth. Because maybe Morah Neetza did tell us, but how am I supposed to know when she's not even talking in English half the time? Another gust of wind blows. Big gray clouds begin to crowd out the sun.

"Oh, well," Mom chirps. "Guess we have a little extra time to run a few errands before football practice." She crunches into her very loud apple and chomps some more. Like it doesn't even cross her mind that maybe I was looking forward to finally, *finally*, getting to the lightsaber, and that this might be my last chance since Rabbi Bob is leaving and is most likely taking his lightsaber with him.

I hate running errands almost as much as I used to hate Hebrew school.

•

I suffer through the post office, the hardware store, and the dry cleaners', but convince Mom to drop me off before I have to get dragged through the shoe store. That place is like a black hole with Mom. We go in, I never know when—or if—we're getting out.

I get to practice five minutes early. Coach is there and players start arriving.

So does the rain.

"Laps, boys!" Coach shouts as he sets up cones around the field. "You're not made out of sugar! A little rain isn't going to melt you!"

I start running and Gideon comes up to join me. "Hey, Avery," he says, panting.

"Hey," I say. I keep my regular pace, and I can tell Gideon is struggling to keep up.

Out of the corner of my eye I see Damon coming up from behind.

Honestly, I don't want to deal with him at all. If Gideon wants to be nice to an evil person, count me out.

I pick up my pace and Gideon can't keep up. From

behind, I hear Damon bark at Gideon, "Outta my way, *dill weed!* Ya loser!"

You'd think by now he'd have come up with something more interesting to say, with so many opportunities to be evil to Gideon.

"Hey, Damon," I hear Gideon cheerfully reply, as if the unfortunate incident at last Sunday's game hadn't even happened. As if none of the unfortunate things between him and Damon ever happened.

My hands clench into a fist as Damon passes me.

Rain is coming down harder. Everyone's head is hanging low and everyone's feet are dragging through the soppy, muddy grass. Coach is sitting on an upside-down bucket under an umbrella.

We all just look like a bunch of losers.

CHAPTER
20

Sunday Morning

"Good morning, young Padawans," Rabbi Bob begins. "It's so nice to see all of your shining faces this morning!"

"My face really *is* shiny this morning!" Little Basha squeals. "Vaseline! I found a whole tub of it this morning in our bathroom!" She circles her small hands across her greasy cheeks. "Makes my skin feel like a real dolphin!"

"May you always be shining, even when you get to be an *alte kocker* like me," Rabbi Bob smiles, then looks down at his hands for a moment. He strokes his beard. "Well, I suppose I should just come out and say it," he finally says, as though he's in the middle of a conversation with himself. "Today is my last day, kids. This whole hiring process went much quicker than I expected. Which is wonderful for you, to have a rabbi at the helm of this starship so soon. But …" his voice trails off "… well, I guess a little bittersweet for me. You people were starting to grow on me, you know?"

What? That's it? He's out of here? For good?

My face starts to feel hot and I'm pretty sure it's because my theory has just been confirmed. Rabbi Bob is nothing but a liar. A faker and a liar. Because why would he leave if he liked us all so much? Nothing but a big, fat liar in front of me and I can't even look at him anymore.

"You're growing on me, too," Little Basha says sadly. She's clearly too little to understand. "Like my favorite wart. It growed here—" she points to a tiny spot on her thumb— "and it stayed for a looooong time, until the doctor freezed it off. It was the best wart I ever had. I wish you didn't get freezed away, too, Rabbi Bob."

"Oh, I'm not getting frozen away," Rabbi Bob assures her. "It's just that, well, my wife and I planned for my retirement this year and ..." Rabbi Bob pauses "... well, we picked the best new rabbi for you, just you wait and see. You'll have a chance to meet the rabbi before you leave today. All I can say is, you are very lucky to have this one."

More words kept coming out of Rabbi Bob's mouth but all I heard was blah, blah, blah. Because why should I waste my time listening to a liar? I've got more important things to worry about, like what kind of evil replacement is going to show up next week. I mean, what kind of person would want to become a rabbi in the first place? Someone who hates science, obviously, and sunlight, and things that are actually interesting. The fact that Rabbi Bob was even semi-tolerable is a total fluke. I can only imagine the dark cave where rabbis are born, filled with dusty old books that I can't understand.

I'm ten years old and I'm trapped in this Hebrew school vortex without Rabbi Bob until my bar mitzvah. That's three more years! Also known as eternity. This makes me feel very clammy and queasy.

Eventually, Rabbi Bob's mouth stops moving and we're released to our Maccabi classrooms, but he stops me just before I go inside. "Avery," he says, "I'm so sorry we didn't have a chance to get to our lightsaber training. I wish I could do it today, but I'm tied up with a luncheon to welcome the new rabbi."

"Whatever."

"I would like a chance to somehow make it up to you. Maybe you could come in for some extra 'tutoring' after school?" He winks and demonstrates a lightsaber maneuver.

"Whatever," I repeat.

•

After one hundred years of my life gets wasted away in Morah Neetza's class, she finally sets us free. Mom isn't here yet. Gideon walks with me toward the bathroom.

We pass by Rabbi Bob's office. The door is open. I see the lightsaber.

I take a peek inside. No one is there.

Without thinking, I say, "Ever see a real lightsaber?"

"A real one? No. Plenty of fakes, though."

"Well, if you want to see a real one," I say, "this may be your last chance." I lead Gideon into Rabbi Bob's office. The little angel on my shoulder suggests that I turn around. "You definitely shouldn't be in Rabbi Bob's office without Rabbi Bob," it says. "And don't even think of touching that lightsaber!"

The little devil disagrees. "You heard the kid," it barks to the little angel, "last chance!"

We quietly step into Rabbi Bob's office. Most of his Star Wars memorabilia is packed into cardboard boxes. The framed poster is still on the wall.

"Hey, that's an original!" Gideon cries.

"No kidding," I whisper back, hoping he starts to whisper, too. No need to call attention to ourselves.

"Check this out," I whisper. I walk up to the lightsaber. The little angel gets flustered. The little devil punches it in the face. "Supposedly, it's real."

With the little angel unconscious, I look out the door to make sure no one is coming. Coast is clear. I carefully lift the lightsaber from its stand. It's exactly as heavy as I remember it.

"Are you sure that's okay to do?" Gideon asks in a fully non-whispering voice. As if he's the little angel on my shoulder now.

"It's fine," I lie. "Rabbi Bob let me do this before." That part is not a lie.

"I don't know, Avery. I kind of feel like we shouldn't be in here touching Rabbi Bob's stuff without Rabbi Bob."

The little angel snaps awake.

Gideon is right. I set the lightsaber back in its stand. "Yeah, we should go."

We take care of our business in the bathroom and head back to class to pack up our things. As we pass Rabbi Bob's office again, I see the lightsaber still sitting there quietly.

Or not so quietly.

Because as I walk by, I'm almost certain I hear it speaking.

You want this, don't you? it says louder than the little angel and the little devil combined.

It is speaking in the deep, haunting voice of Emperor Palpatine.

"Did you hear that?" I ask Gideon.

"Hear what?"

"Oh, nothing. Never mind." Gideon keeps walking, but my feet stop. "I left something in the bathroom," I blurt out. It's another lie. "You go ahead. I'll see you at football." Gideon disappears down the hall.

I take a step closer to the lightsaber.

Take your Jedi weapon. Use it, it says.

I look around. It's just me, and the lightsaber. I gently close the door behind me.

Give in to your anger, it tells me forcefully.

Somehow, I am standing before the lightsaber.

Somehow, my hands are wrapped around the hilt.

I hear Emperor Palpatine's voice. *It is unavoidable. It is your destiny.*

Somehow, I am lifting the lightsaber from its stand.

Somehow, I am turning it on. The red blade glows to life.

I scan my eyes across Rabbi Bob's office, all packed up in boxes.

I picture the new rabbi, a zombie-like creature whose only purpose in life is to make us believe things we don't want to believe and tell us stories that aren't true. I picture my parents, willingly sacrificing *three more years* of my life to this creature, probably even smiling as they do it. Twice a week for about a million more weeks, with no Rabbi Bob. No weird jokes. No oddball instruments. No surprising Star Wars references. No one to understand that I am a man of science. Just a zombie covered in worm holes threatening to turn me into a little Jewish scholar.

I clench every muscle in my body and raise the lightsaber over my head. I feel the massive hum vibrate through me.

Something else flashes before me.

Evil Damon, and he's picking on Gideon.

I see myself, too afraid to stop him.

I see Gideon just taking it. And worse, being nice.

Then I think about losing every game.

I begin to move the lightsaber. I know how to do it, I think. I've seen all the movies 400 times.

I swing to the right. The hum rises. It feels great.

"I've only been dreaming about playing on a real football team basically all my life," I say out loud, to no one. I swing to the left. The hum falls. "And I finally convince my parents to let me play, for one measly year."

I circle it over my head. I am beginning to sweat. "So now I'm on a team, and what happens?"

I slice through the air diagonally. "We lose every game!"

I spin, the hum circles around me. "As if that isn't bad enough! There's Damon—the evil Sith!" I picture his ugly face all curled up and sneering the words *dill weed* and *loser*. I cut through the air straight ahead of me. My heart is pounding a new rhythm. The hum gets louder. All that ballroom dancing in PE that I thought for sure was a big waste of time suddenly feels useful as I begin to maneuver the lightsaber more gracefully, dipping and twirling in the close quarters of Rabbi Bob's office. I cannot stop.

Damon's ugly face is floating before me and I am in battle against him, saying everything I wish I could have said to his real face.

"Leave Gideon alone! He's my friend! And I'm sorry that I never got to know him before, but I know him now! Like I know he's the worst player on the team and I don't even care. And he's into Star Wars and his grandfather is a Hungarian pirate with a dirty mouth—which is completely awesome!"

I leap and land in a crouched position. "I know that Gideon is weird, like good weird, like interesting weird, like nobody else I know. I've been too much of a wimp to stop you from picking on him, Darth Damon, like a real friend would." I spring up and holler, "Yeah, that's right! I'm admitting it! I think I could have a friend like Gideon, even if he's from Hebrew school."

I hoist the lightsaber over my head. I can feel my lungs expanding with every breath and blood racing hot through my veins. "And you know what else I'm not too afraid to admit? For the first time in my life I actually sort of, kind of, semi-like Hebrew school!" I twirl the lightsaber in a perfect figure-eight. "But Rabbi Bob is leaving, and then what?!"

I spin fast on my heels. "So take that!" I shout and a wave of energy is released as I jab the lightsaber into Darth Damon's pug face before me.

But I underestimate the distance between me and the framed original Star Wars poster from 1977 hanging on the wall.

It comes crashing down. The glass plate shatters into a million pieces.

I am drenched in sweat and completely out of breath. Which is why, when the door swings open and I hear Morah Neetza scream, I don't know what to do. "What in ze world are you doing 'ere, Avery?!" I have a hard time answering.

I drop the lightsaber. It thunks and cracks like a small death. The red blade disappears. The humming chokes and then stops. There is nothing but silence and Morah Neetza scowling at me with her arms crossed over her sparkly sweatshirt. "I do not find zis kind of monkey beezness very amusing. Zis is a synagogue, not a zoo!" she scorns. For all the times I've seen Morah Neetza frown, I've never actually seen her angry. The sight is terrifying. "*What*, exactly, are you doing 'ere?" she repeats.

Rabbi Bob comes running up to us. He picks up the lightsaber and tries to start it. Nothing happens. He takes a look at me, the dead lightsaber, and the shattered frame. He tugs at his beard. "Oy," he says.

"Avery," Morah Neetza says sternly without taking her eyes off me, "would you care to explain to ze nice rabbi what you are doing 'ere?"

I can feel my face turning bright red and my stomach twisting into a jumbled knot. Even though my best option is probably to remain silent, I hear my quivering voice say, "The thing is, Morah Neetza, I've never known what I was doing here."

•

I am awkwardly standing in the hallway in between Morah Neetza, who I'm pretty sure is going to kill me with her scowl, and Rabbi Bob.

"Do you know what zey would 'ave done to me when I was in school if I 'ad tried such monkey beezness?" Morah Neetza snaps. "Zey would 'ave made me schlep rocks across ze playground for ze rest of ze year. Except zat we didn't 'ave a fancy-shmancy playground like you 'ave in America. We 'ad a field made from flat 'ard dirt. Zat's what we 'ad. And zey would 'ave made me schlep rocks from one end to ze uhzer, to teach me to behave like a civilized 'uman, not like a wild monkey." Morah Neetza jabs her finger in my direction.

"Yes, I understand, Morah Neetza," Rabbi Bob says patiently. "And while I believe there is value in the methods from your childhood—shall we say, tough love?—I'm not sure that would be an appropriate punishment for this particular crime." Rabbi Bob looks at me, then back at Morah Neetza.

The fates seem to be undecided. Either I will be allowed to go with my mom, who is in the lobby waiting to take me to my football game, or I will have to stay and schlep rocks over dirt for the rest of the afternoon, and possibly for the rest of my Hebrew school life.

"You see, Morah Neetza, I did give Avery permission to be in my office," Rabbi Bob lies. "We've been working together in my office on a particular project for a few weeks now, and I'm sure Avery was just putting on the finishing touches." He looks at me knowingly, and I am immediately aware that this is the man who is going to simultaneously get me to my game almost on time while saving me from the wrath of Morah Neetza, who is sucking food out of her teeth while giving me a major stink eye. He smiles at me. "It's no big deal, really. We'll get that all cleaned up in no time. Do you know where the broom closet is, Avery?"

I nod, stunned.

He continues, "Run along and grab the broom and dustpan. I know you have an important event to go to, so let's make it quick."

Morah Neetza pats her spongy hair and puts her hand on her hip. "Everyone is too nice in America," she sighs, "but you are ze boss, Rabbi." She turns and walks away, muttering, "Always smiling and making ze nice nice in America."

"I'm sorry I broke your picture," I whisper to Rabbi Bob as I sweep a gazillion shards of broken glass into the dustpan he's holding. "And your lightsaber."

"Nonsense. And besides, you had some impressive maneuvers in there. Are you sure you've never trained with a lightsaber before?"

My jaw drops. "Did you …" I begin to ask. "Were you … I mean … watching … I thought I was alone … why didn't … why did you let me …?"

"One should never interrupt The Force at work, Avery," he says softly. "Now, get going before you completely miss your game."

CHAPTER
21

Sunday Afternoon

By the time I get to the field, the score is seven to zero, Seahawks in the lead. I see Coach and the Bears on the sideline for a time out. Gideon squeezes over to make room for me in the circle.

"The Seahawks are good, but not unbeatable," Coach says. "You get to work, Bears, and we have a shot." We all put our hands in the middle of the huddle. But before we break out, Coach lifts up his feet and checks the bottoms of his shoes. "Everybody, check your shoes," he says. "Smells like one of us stepped in dog poo." He's right. It does. Still shoulder to shoulder, we all lift up our feet and check the bottoms of our shoes. Nothing turns up.

"All right then," Coach says. "Go, Bears!" we chant.

Gideon takes a small detour to his backpack under the bench. "Psst, Avery," he calls to me in a raspy whisper. He waves me over and unzips his backpack. Inside, is Potion

#18. "Put some of this on the back of your helmet," he whispers as he opens the vial. He dabs some on my helmet. The smell is so strong I want to throw up. "It'll keep the other team away."

"Is that what Coach was smelling?" I ask. "I thought it was a familiar scent."

Gideon nods. "I think it's working. No one has even come close to me. It's like a force field."

•

Five minutes to go before half time. We've successfully kept the Seahawks from scoring and now it's second down and ten, Bears in possession at the forty-yard line.

"Avery, Gideon," Coach barks, "you're both in."

We jog onto the field to replace the outgoing players.

The center hikes the ball to Sean, who looks downfield toward Damon, who is supposed to receive it. Sean sends the ball flying downfield, but his aim is completely off and the ball is headed more or less in my direction. Strangely, no one is on me, so I race to the spot where the ball is going to land and get there just in time.

Perfect catch.

I run like my life depends on it.

Past the thirty … past the twenty … still no one is on me.

Past the ten … touchdown!

I can't believe this! Best feeling ever!

All the Bears are hollering and fist bumping each other. Morale is so out of Challenger Deep!

A familiar voice shouts from the stands, "Atta boy! Would you look at that! Edelman in the making!" I turn around to see Rabbi Bob standing and clapping. "Atta boy, Avery!" he calls to me.

Rabbi Bob is here, in the stands? In the minute it takes me to compute this, we run a play for a PAT, or point after touchdown and complete it. "Go, Bears!" Rabbi Bob shouts even louder.

I discreetly wave to him. He points to the scoreboard and gives me two thumbs-up. Tied at seven. We actually have a chance of winning this game.

I look back at the stands and see Rabbi Bob giving a high five to my parents and to Yapa, who is there in his rainbow Sherpa hat with a cigar dangling from his smiling mouth.

The only non-Seahawk person not happy about our undeniable turnaround is Darth Damon's Dad. "THAT WAS YOURS, D!" he screams from the stands. He charges off like an angry toddler who didn't get his way.

With Darth Damon's Dad gone, this means we don't have to listen to his evil commentary running in the background for the rest of the game. Massive relief. Plus, I've got Mom, Dad, Yapa and Rabbi Bob on our side.

Ever have that tingling, lucky feeling that things are going to go your way? Like you might actually win a football game before the season is over?

•

During half time we slurp down Gatorade and listen to Coach run through our offensive starting lineup for the third quarter. Ref blows the whistle and we all get into position. I have butterflies banging into the walls of my gut, but it only adds to my overall excited feeling that victory is within reach.

"Go, Bears!" I hear Rabbi Bob shout. Inside my helmet, I am smiling.

•

Ten minutes into the second half and—because Gideon takes a hit from a huge oncoming Seahawk for me—I score a *second* touchdown! Thirteen to seven! We are actually in the lead!

Coach pulls me and Gideon out. "Nice work, Avery," he says and gives me a pat on the back. "Take a break, kid. You worked hard." I stay next to Coach but Gideon sits on the bench. "Gideon, you okay?" he asks. "That looked like a rough tackle."

"Sure, I'm okay," Gideon says. He takes off his helmet and holds his head in his hands for a second. He shakes it off and repeats, "Yep, all good here."

Coach looks around, sniffing the air around him. He turns to me with a confused look on his face. "Buddy, check your shoes again, would you?"

I lift my feet up and check the bottoms, but I know it's not my shoes.

It's my force field.

I sit next to Gideon, who's holding his head again. "Who needs a lightsaber when you've got Potion #18?" I say. He nods back at me like he knows we're going to win, too.

•

Seahawks start off with the ball, but after a wicked interception by our strong safety, we get possession.

We keep the ball going down the line, play by play, until we get to the Seahawks' thirty-yard line, first and ten. I don't know what happened to the old Bears, but these new Bears are kicking the Seahawks' butts. It feels like I'm watching a perfectly oiled machine with all the parts doing exactly the right things, play after play. We are totally going to take this.

Our center snaps the ball back to Sean, who avoids a deadly sack and miraculously manages to throw a perfect spiral downfield. This time, Damon is in place, ready to receive it. He makes a perfect catch, then outruns the Seahawks' safety. My heart is racing and my cheeks are burning from whatever goofy smile my face can't seem to stop making.

There is only one problem.

And it comes fast in the form of a Seahawk cornerback. The fast one no one saw coming.

He races up to Damon as Damon closes in on the Seahawks' ten-yard line. He pounds into him and Damon takes a hard fall. Damon curls himself around the ball as a herd of Seahawk defenders pile on top of him. Which is totally against league rules. Ref blows the whistle and the timer stops. One by one, players get up until they are all standing but one. Damon. Who is still curled around the ball.

Gideon and I leap off the bench at the same time, but he trips over. He gets up quickly, holding his head again. "You sure you're okay?" I ask, but he's already racing down the sideline toward Damon with all the other players. Damon is rocking back and forth on the ground with one arm gripped on the ball, the other reaching toward his ankle. All of us Bears have circled around as Coach kneels down beside Damon and takes off his helmet. His extremely spiky faux hawk now looks floppy and gooey.

Damon is crying. Hard.

"Go away, idiots!" he screams.

Everyone backs off. Except for one.

Gideon inches in closer. "Are you deaf?" Damon shouts. "Leave me alone!" he sobs. But Gideon doesn't. He picks up Damon's helmet. Coach lifts Damon off the ground and wraps his arms around his waist. Damon's face is covered in tears. Gideon stays right by Damon's side as Coach guides him, hobbling toward the bench. I'm trailing right behind them, not sure what to do.

Coach sets Damon down on the bench. Gideon races into the stands, still carrying Damon's helmet. He quickly returns with Yapa. Rabbi Bob is beside him, too.

Yapa says to Coach, "I'm a medic. Let me take a look at the boy's leg."

"Yapa was a medic?" I quietly ask Gideon.

"Yep, at sea. Kind of like the school nurse, but on a cargo ship." I notice that Gideon is squinting his eyes like it's too bright outside, even though the sky is dark gray.

Rabbi Bob puts his hand on my shoulder and leans in to ask, "Might this be the evil Sith you battled in my office?" He nods his head toward Damon.

"That's the one," I whisper back.

"I had the good fortune of sitting beside his father. I noticed he left quite angrily after your touchdown."

Players start crowding around. The ref comes over to have a word with Coach. "This man is a medic. He'll take a look," Coach tells her. In all the commotion, Coach nods to Yapa. "Thanks," he says.

Yapa carefully kneels beside Damon's bad ankle, which has now swollen to the size of a softball. He gently places his hands on Damon's leg. Damon scrunches his face in pain and cries like a baby. Gideon leans over Damon and tells him, "Yapa will take care of you."

"The boy needs to get to the emergency room," Yapa says to Coach as he wraps a cold pack from Coach's first-aid kit around Damon's ankle.

"Let me call his father," Coach replies.

After a minute, he comes back to Yapa. "No answer. And I can't leave the rest of the players." Coach looks at

Damon, who is sobbing. "Go ahead, take him in, I'll keep trying to reach his dad."

Yapa and Gideon flank Damon and together they lift him off the bench.

My feet don't move. I don't know what to do.

Gideon turns to me. "Come with us," he says, "We'll need your help." But I remain stuck.

Rabbi Bob looks me in the eye. "Your friend needs you," he says. "Go. I'll tell your parents to meet you at the emergency room."

CHAPTER
22

Damon cries the whole way to the emergency room. Crying like I never saw a kid cry. Crying like someone turned on a faucet in his eyes. His face is puffy and red and covered in slobber. Every couple of minutes Gideon, who is sitting next to Damon in the back seat, hands him a tissue. Damon honks his nose into every single one.

Yapa is driving. He elbows me with a bag of red chips. "You need a nosh?" he asks. "All this cryin' is makin' me hungry."

Just a whiff from the bag tells me they're going to be crazy spicy. Yapa laughs at me. "Siracha," he says. "It'll put hair on your chest."

"No, thanks," I say. Yapa pops a handful in his mouth. Yapa must have a very hairy chest.

He pulls right up to the entrance of the emergency room. He hops out and comes to Damon's side of the car.

Just like on the field, Yapa and Gideon flank Damon and

they walk him to the registration desk. The receptionist gives us a clipboard with some papers to fill out and tells us to have a seat.

"Boys," Yapa says, "I'll go park the car. Back in a jiff."

Gideon is sandwiched between me and Damon in the waiting room. "Listen, Damon," he says, "let's fill out these forms while we're waiting for the doctor, okay?"

Damon honks his nose into his sleeve and nods.

Since I'm holding the clipboard and pen, I figure I'll do the writing.

"Full name?" Gideon reads over my shoulder.

Damon sniffles and says, "Damon Ungus Diggens."

Damon Ungus Diggens, I write. D.U.D. His initials spell "dud." Maybe this is part of Damon's anger issue. I start to giggle as I write his name, but Gideon shakes his head at me. I hold back.

"Mother's name?" Gideon continues.

"Don't have one," Damon mutters and wipes his tears with the back of his snotty sleeve.

"Everyone has a mother," I point out. "We just need to write her name down."

"Hmm. You don't have a mother … and I don't have a father," Gideon says, leaning in. "Maybe that's something we have in common. We're both from a one-parent family."

I'm about to explain that, technically, everyone has a mother and a father, but I don't, because, well, I never knew that Gideon didn't have a father.

I guess I never knew that Damon didn't have a mother, either.

It's feeling very hard for me to believe that Damon and Gideon have anything in common, but here's Gideon, pointing out that they do. And I don't know why he is, but I can see Damon looking up at him and, for the first time since the accident, stops crying.

"She left us when I was a baby," Damon mumbles. His eyes are bloodshot and snot is dripping from his nose. For a Sith, he's looking pretty pathetic.

I start scanning the form for the place to write this information down but there isn't a designated spot. I guess the form doesn't need to know.

Then Gideon says, "My mom had me when she was kind of old. She said she didn't have time to wait for a husband to come along."

"That's weird," Damon says, but not in an evil way, just honest. I never heard his voice sound so … normal.

Yapa appears out of nowhere. "Got the car parked," he announces. "And what's weird?"

"That Mom didn't want to wait for a husband to come along before she had me," Gideon answers.

"That's my girl," Yapa says proudly. "A chip off the old block. Knows what she wants, knows how to get it, doesn't let no one stop her." Yapa smiles broadly. Without a cigar dangling from his mouth, I notice the huge gap between his front teeth for the first time. Like you could drive a truck through it. He beams at Gideon. "And look what she brought into this world!" he says a little too loudly. "The best!"

He looks more carefully at Gideon. "Why is there a lump on the side of your head, kid?" he asks. I look more carefully, too. There is a lump on the side of his head.

"It's nothing," he answers dismissively.

"Nothing, my *tukkhes*," Yapa replies inspecting the lump more closely.

A nurse comes through a side door pushing an empty wheelchair and wheels it up to us. "I'm guessing you're Damon," he says to Damon. "How about we take a look at that ankle of yours?" he says sweetly.

He hoists Damon into the wheelchair. "Want to come along, Grandpa?" he asks Yapa. "Looks like your boy needs an extra dose of love."

Yapa doesn't correct the nurse. He just tosses up his hands and says, "No problemo!"

The nurse spins the wheelchair around. Yapa tells me to get an icepack for Gideon from the nurses' station, then joins Damon and the nurse as they walk through the sliding electric doors. Just before the doors close behind them, Damon glances back at Gideon and gives a small wave.

Gideon whispers to me, "Looks kind of like a lost puppy, doesn't he?"

"It's strange, but he does."

And all this time I thought he was a Sith.

•

I go to the nurses' station, like Yapa said, to get Gideon an ice pack. The nurse also gives me two cups of apple juice with teeny-tiny straws and extra ice, and a bunch of cracker packs, which I stuff in my pocket.

"Here, put this on your lump," I say. I set the cups of apple juice down on a small table.

"Thank you." He reaches for the juice and slurps a sip. "Have you ever noticed that drinks taste better through teeny-tiny straws?" Gideon winces a little as he presses the ice pack to the side of his head.

"It hurts?" I ask.

"Not too bad. Nothing compared to Damon's ankle."

"Did you get that when the Seahawk crashed into you?"

Gideon nods.

"Thanks," I say. "I couldn't have made that touchdown if you hadn't blocked him for me."

"I bet you could have."

I look at him sitting there, kind of folded over in a doughy sort of way, one plump hand curled around the ice pack, the other cradling the cup of juice. Gideon, who cried over a dead bug in second grade. Gideon, who struggles to run laps around the football field and takes the ball in the wrong direction, and gets in everyone's way. He really is the worst player on the team. Maybe even in the whole league.

"You been into football for a long time?" I ask.

"Nah," he says.

"How come you joined EBFL then?"

He lowers the ice pack and takes a sip of juice. The lump

on the side of his head is shining bright red. "I like to try new things," he says.

"Yeah, but football is kind of a rough sport. And you're not really …" I don't know how to finish my thought without insulting Gideon.

"A great athlete?" he finishes for me. He presses the ice back on his lump.

"I guess. Sort of," I say, even though what I'm thinking is: *Exactly.*

"Yeah, I know. But I thought it would be worth a try. Yapa always says, *You only get one life, might as well live it.*" Gideon looks up at me. "I'm also an excellent eavesdropper and spy," he adds.

"What do you mean?"

"You're not the only one who overheard Damon talking to Jaxon at the end of math class that day, when he said there were new football times. And you left the EBFL screen page open on Mr. S's computer. It was pretty obvious you were going to sign up."

"You did it because I was doing it?"

Gideon doesn't answer right away. He lowers the ice pack again and takes another sip of juice. Then he says, "We've been together in Hebrew school ever since kindergarten. But I'm new at your regular school. I don't know too many kids there. You never really talked to me so I thought maybe if I joined—"

"It's not that I didn't want to be friends with you," I jump in. "It's just that … I like to keep Hebrew school separate.

You know, like nuts and chocolate-chip cookies. They don't taste right mixed together."

Gideon tilts his head to the side like he's questioning something. Reminds me of the ewok Wicket, when he first meets Princess Leia in *Return of the Jedi*. "Nah."

"Nah? What do you mean, 'Nah'?"

"I mean it's probably too late. It's already mixed together."

"What do you mean, 'It's probably too late' and 'It's already mixed together'?" I feel like a dorky parrot repeating everything Gideon is saying.

"I mean we've been together in Hebrew school a long time. And I don't think you can spend so much time in one place without at least a little bit of it getting mixed in somehow." He lowers the ice pack from his head. "You're here with me right now, and I'm from Hebrew school. See what I mean?" He smirks and adds, "I really like nuts in my chocolate-chip cookies."

"Right, but …" I try to think of what to say but the truth is I don't know what to think.

Gideon lifts his hand to put the ice pack back on his lump but chooses the wrong hand. Apple juice from his cup pours down his back. We look at each other and start to crack up. "Finally!" I burst out, "You're not spilling on me!"

Just then the electric doors to the waiting room slide open. "Do you have my son?" a man barks. Startled, Gideon spins around to see who it is and, in the process of the spinning, spills the remainder of his juice in my lap. Slightly stunned and yet not totally surprised, I grab a handful of napkins as we watch Damon's dad barge in. I can hear the Imperial March playing in the background as I mop up my lap. Damon's dad storms up to the nurses' station. "Do you have my son?" he repeats.

"I'm sorry, sir," the nurse replies, "you'll have to be a little more specific than that."

"My son, Damon. I got a call from his coach saying he got hurt and some old man brought him here."

"You mean the boy with the injured ankle and his grandfather?"

"He doesn't have a grandfather," his dad says. "And yeah, the coach said something in his message about an ankle. You have him here?"

"Yes, sir, we do. Your son fractured his ankle. The doctor is treating him now."

"What time did he get here? How long has he been at the hospital? This is insane! I stepped away from the game because I had to make a few calls for work and next thing I know a total stranger is taking my kid away, pretending to be his grandfather!"

"He was injured, sir. I believe the elderly gentleman was helping your son get the care he needed," the nurse says, trying to be polite.

"Yeah, well how about you turn around and come back to find *your* kid missing. Then we can talk. My boy is all I got. Do you understand me? Scary as heck, when you can't find your kid."

Damon's dad scared? Didn't see that one coming.

"Why don't you have a seat, sir?" the nurse says softly. "The doctor will come out to speak with you when she's done."

"He better be okay is all I'm saying," his dad grumbles as he takes a seat across from Gideon and me. We watch as he nervously flips through the channels on the TV in the corner until he gets to a football game. Rams versus Broncos.

"Do you like it?" I ask Gideon.

"Like what?"

"Football. You know, now that you're on the Bears."

"It's not too bad," he says. "But I could do without the senseless brutality."

I think about all the times Damon was so evil to Gideon. I lower my voice and ask, "How come you ran to help Damon? I mean, don't you think he kind of deserved it? You know, for always being so mean to you?"

Damon's dad starts loudly coaching players on the screen.

Gideon shrugs. "I guess I didn't think that much about it. I just knew that his dad wasn't there and he was really hurt. I'm sure you would have done the same thing if I didn't do it first."

I can feel the little devil on my shoulder looking away, embarrassed. Because he knows I wouldn't have.

•

Gideon and I keep busy in the ER waiting room by eating cracker packs, slurping apple juice refills through teeny-tiny straws, and asking each other Star Wars trivia questions.

Me: What Imperial Star Destroyer intercepted Princess Leia's ship above Tatooine in *A New Hope*?

Gideon: The *Devastator*. How many engines are on an X-wing fighter?

Me: Four. What planet was Obi-Wan Kenobi born on?

Gideon: Stewjon. Who was Obi-Wan's Jedi Master?

Me: Too easy. Qui-Gon Jinn. According to Yoda, who must Luke face in order to complete his training?

Gideon smiles and lifts his eyebrows. "Darth Damon."

"Ha, ha. Very funny."

Me: Okay, ready for another one? Good luck with this—What's the name of the X-wing attack force that Luke Skywalker joins during the Battle of Yavin in Episode IV?

Gideon: Red Squadron.

"Man, you're good," I say because, well, he is. Crazy good, as a matter of fact.

Gideon: The surviving members from Red Squadron later appear in *The Empire Strikes Back*. What is the name of their group?

I never thought this day would come, that someone could stump me on Star Wars trivia. I scrunch up my face, simultaneously hoping the answer comes and wondering why people scrunch up their faces when they're thinking hard.

"Give up?" Gideon asks.

"Never. But I will take a hint."

"Think of a standalone Star Wars movie."

"*Rogue One*?"

"Close."

I scrunch my face harder. Got it. "Rogue Squadron!"

"Right!" Gideon says.

The doors that Damon and Yapa went through slide back open and a doctor in blue scrubs comes out. Luckily, it's after I got the answer. She walks right up to us.

"Gideon? Avery?" she asks.

We both nod.

"Hi, boys. Your grandfather told me I'd find you here," she says. "I just want to let you know that your friend is going to be just fine. Yapa is sitting with him while he rests. Damon fractured his ankle, but I was able to set it. Everything is back in place." She smiles. "I even put a beautiful green cast on him that all his friends at school can sign."

All his friends? I'm thinking about how short that list is when Damon's dad stomps up to the doctor. "You have Damon?"

The doctor looks a little startled. "And you are?"

"I'm his father, that's who I am. And no one asked for my permission. Where is he? Is he okay? I want to see him."

"My apologies, sir, but we had to treat him immediately."

"I had to leave the game to take a call from work," Damon's dad snaps. "And since I can't be two places at once I guess I missed the accident. I can't do it all! Where's Damon? Is he okay?"

"Yes, sir, he'll be fine. I was just telling Damon's friends that he fractured his ankle, but that I was able to successfully set it. I put him in a cast that will need to stay on for four to six weeks. He'll need to use crutches during that time as the injured leg cannot bear any weight. But we were able to avoid surgery, so that's great."

"You telling me he's out for the rest of the season?" Damon's dad asks.

"If you're referring to the football season, then yes, he'll be out."

"I don't see what's so great about that. I had him on track to get a scholarship to Notre Dame Prep. Best high-school football team in the state."

The doctor looks confused. "But your son is eleven years old," she says, "don't you think he has time?"

"You think there's just a tree that grows an endless supply of football scholarships to that school?" Damon's dad says defensively. "If you don't get them trained properly and noticed early, you might as well forget about getting a scholarship to Notre Dame Prep. And we can't afford the school without one. So you'll have to forgive me if I'm not jumping for joy that my son is out for the season."

"Sir, I may not understand your plan for your son,

but I do understand his fracture. Young children have tremendous resilience and a remarkable way of recovering from injury, so much faster than us grown-ups. Damon will be good as new by the start of winter, and stronger than ever when the next football season rolls around. So I don't believe you need to worry, you'll get your star player back." She glances over to us and back to Damon's dad. "Do any of you have questions?"

"When can I see him?" Damon's dad asks.

"The nurse just needs to finish some paperwork to discharge him from the hospital, but you're welcome to go in the recovery room. All of you are."

The doctor settles her eyes on Gideon. "You're Gideon, right?" She focuses on the lump on his head. "Looks like you got a good bump there. Mind if I take a closer look at that?"

She gently presses her fingers on the side of his head. He scrunches his face like it hurts. "You got this from football, too?" she asks. Gideon nods. "Rough game today, huh? Headache?" she asks.

"Not much."

"Will you do me a favor, Gideon?" she asks. "Make sure to see your doctor about that first thing tomorrow morning. I'll talk to your grandfather so he understands it's important to take you in. I'm sure it's fine, but I'll feel a lot better knowing you had it checked out by your regular doctor. Sound like a plan?"

Gideon nods. The doctor leads the three of us down

a hall to a small room with a big bed. Damon is sitting with his green-casted leg propped up on a pile of pillows. Yapa is in a chair beside him with a wet, unlit cigar dangling from the corner of his mouth. His hands are outstretched in front of him and he's talking like he's in the middle of a story.

"This big, I'm telling ya! That fish was *this big*! And there's no way I'm gonna let her go, right? So what do I do? I grab a fishing net and blade, throw off my shoes and jump in the water! I don't care there's chunks of ice floating around. That was a prize fish tangled up in the line! I'd be a darned fool to let that one go!" Yapa holds on to his belly as he laughs like crazy. I'm wondering how the cigar doesn't fall out. "The boys on deck are peering over like I'm about to become shark bait, but I just keep my eyes on the prize. I wrangle the fish into the net—whoa, Nellie, she was a wild one!—and cut the line. Just before I reach the boat ladder, I hold up that great silver beauty and call up to the crew—their jaws have hit the deck by now—'Rub-a-dub-dub, happy man in the tub!'" Yapa looks like he's going to bust, he's laughing so hard. Damon is laughing, too. Must be contagious because when I look over my shoulder, I see Damon's dad's face cracking into something like a grin. Yapa slaps Damon on the arm. "Now that's what I call a good day of fishing!"

Yapa looks up and sees us in the doorway. He flashes a huge smile. "Come on in, boys—the water is fine! Me and my friend Damon here are just shootin' the breeze!"

CHAPTER
23

Monday

Gideon is not at school today. Not staring out the window in first period homeroom, not chewing his pencil in language arts, not getting turned around in the hallway, not sitting by himself in the cafeteria, not spilling anything on me, not awkwardly stuffing papers into his backpack in math at the end of the day. Even though I know he's not at school, I keep looking around for him, half expecting him to be. Reminds me of the big, old armchair we used to have in the corner our living room. It was always there, but then one day I came home and it was gone and the room suddenly felt empty.

•

"Gideon wasn't at school today," I tell my parents at dinner that night.

"Yes, I know," Mom says. "His mother came into the bank this morning. We chatted for a few minutes. She said she brought Gideon in to the doctor this morning to look at that bump on his head."

"Is he okay?"

"They suspect he has a mild concussion." She doesn't say it, but I can hear in Mom's voice a *see-I-told-you-so* kind of thing.

"A mild concussion? But he seemed totally fine after the game," I argue. "I mean, we took Damon to the ER and everything. He was walking fine. We even played Star Wars trivia in the waiting room and he got every answer right. He definitely wouldn't get every answer right if he had a concussion. How would he know the name of the Imperial Star Destroyer that intercepted Princess Leia's ship above Tatooine if he had a concussion? If he had a concussion, wouldn't he be unconscious or something?"

"Whoa, Avery. Take a breath," Dad says. "And not necessarily. With concussions, there's a range, from mild to severe."

"And his is mild?"

Mom nods. "Apparently he had a headache all day yesterday and into the night. So they told him to take it extra easy this week. No school and, obviously, no football."

I look at my plate of food. The thought of eating suddenly makes me want to puke. "Is he going to be okay?"

"He'll be fine, Avery," Dad assures me. "They're just keeping him home as a precaution to make sure that, if it is a mild concussion, his brain has a chance to fully recover."

I sit at the table with a head full of thoughts but no more words to say. If he had a headache all day yesterday, why didn't he say something? Why did he take care of Damon—who isn't even his friend—if he was hurting?

I remember asking him. *How come you ran to help Damon? I mean, don't you think he kind of deserved it? You know, for always being so mean to you?*

And I think about his answer. *I guess I didn't think that much about it. I just knew that his dad wasn't there and he was really hurt. I'm sure you would have done the same thing if I didn't do it first.*

I hear Gideon's voice saying this to me but … I don't know. I push bits of food around on my plate. It just doesn't make any sense. Damon is a mean, horrible person who bullies everyone around, especially Gideon—he totally deserved to get his butt kicked. There are good guys, and there are bad guys, and the good guys are not supposed to help the bad guys. That's just the way it is.

Good luck getting killed, gill weed. Ya loser. I can hear Damon's stupid voice ringing in my ears. I see him tripping Gideon; knocking off his helmet and teasing him; walking away after ramming him on purpose during practice. I see Gideon's nose swollen to the size of a bagel.

Damon is a bad guy who fights good guys, just like he's made to do.

So why does Gideon keep being nice to him? The

question is circling in my head like a hamster in a wheel and I can't get off it. As soon as Gideon is better, we will need to discuss.

I really hope he gets better soon.

Mom and Dad are chatting away about I don't know what—it just sounds like droning background noise. I don't want to eat anything on my plate. I take a sip of water, but even that feels hard to swallow.

Another voice rings in my ears. *YOU GONNA BE A WINNER OR A LOSER, SON?* Damon's dad. Shouting at the games; insulting referees; throwing his weight around like he's the boss of everyone. If I were Damon, I'd be so embarrassed. The dude's a bad guy.

In case you haven't noticed, that kid is pure evil. And from the looks of it, his evilness might be genetic, I had said to Gideon.

The picture of Damon crying like a baby in the back seat of Yapa's car flashes in my mind, catching me by surprise. The picture of Damon waving to Gideon as he got wheeled into the ER follows. He did look like a lost puppy. And I hear Gideon's reply: *Evilness isn't like eye color, Avery. You don't just inherit it.*

But what about Star Wars? Does this mean every Sith just *learned* how to be a Sith? That the Siths all started out as good guys? It doesn't seem possible. But then I remember something. Some of the Siths *did* start out as good guys. Like Count Dooku, Darth Vader, and Kylo Ren. They all started as Jedi.

"Everything okay, Avery?" I hear Mom ask, but her

voice is fuzzy in the background. "You're hardly touching your dinner."

"I'm fine. Just not that hungry." Nothing is adding up right in my head. "Okay if I go to my lab for a little while?"

•

I start out mixing potions. Tropical-scented wood cleaner, unrefrigerated milk, and tea tree oil. I stir it all around in my beaker until the fragrance begins to sting my nose. Pretty offensive, all right. I pour the liquid into a small vial, cap it, stick a piece of masking tape on it, and label it: Potion #19. I open the drawer where I keep my cache of stinky potions. They're all there, lined up. But …

… What's the point? I mean, what am I going to do with nineteen vials of vomit-inducing potions?

I pick up the one labeled "Potion #18." I remember the day I gave some to Gideon.

You can keep it, I said.

Really?

Sure. I have another vial at home.

Wow. Thanks, Avery. This is the second-best thing anyone has ever given me.

I flop onto my bean bag chair next to my pile of science books. They're supposed to go on the bookshelf Mom put down here, but I find the pile system so much more efficient. I randomly pick up a book. *What Are the Odds?*

A Kid's Introduction to Statistics. I bought it back when I was thinking about becoming a professional poker player.

I turn to the first page and start to read, but my mind wanders ... I shake up the vial of Potion #18 and watch the contents settle ... what are the odds of there being someone who loves stinky potions as much as me? Pretty slim, right? After all, they're stinky. And then I think about the odds of knowing this person practically my whole life and never finding out that he loves stinky potions as much as I do. I mean, if Gideon hadn't eavesdropped on me eavesdropping on the conversation between Damon and Jaxon, and if I hadn't left the EBFL page open, and if Gideon hadn't done his detective work, then he wouldn't have signed up for football. Then we could have conceivably just trudged along in Hebrew school and regular school, side by side like two parallel lines that never intersect or share a passion for stinky potions.

I shake up the vial of Potion #18 again. What are the odds that it really worked as a force field when Gideon smeared it on our helmets? Was it a coincidence that *that* was the day I made my first touchdown? If Gideon hadn't blocked the Seahawk, I definitely wouldn't have made my second touchdown. And then he wouldn't be stuck at home with a concussion.

"Avery!" Dad calls down. "Time for bed! It's getting late and you have a long day tomorrow!"

"Coming!" I shout. I slog up the stairs carrying the statistics book. Tomorrow is Tuesday. Hebrew school. I remember that Rabbi Bob had his last day last week, so he won't be there. And neither will Gideon. I suddenly don't feel very well as I consider my odds of surviving alone in a black hole.

That night in bed I flip through the pages of my statistics book and wonder if reading it will help me calculate an answer.

CHAPTER

24

Tuesday Afternoon

"Well, *shalom*, Avery!" a voice booms as I slowly enter the sanctuary, late as usual. I can't help it if Mother Nature still happens to call every Tuesday afternoon at 3:59. Plus, the triple wash with soap takes time.

I look up and see Rabbi Bob on the *bimah*.

Wait. What? *Rabbi Bob?*

"Don't look so surprised to see me, young Padawan! You know, you're going to have to work a lot harder to get rid of me!"

"What the … I mean, I thought … you were … a goner."

Rabbi Bob's laughter feels strangely like a glitter shower. "True, I'm not a young man anymore but I didn't think I was so close to the grave! Jeesh! A goner?" With two fingers, Rabbi Bob checks his pulse at his neck. "I'm afraid I'm still very much alive. *Baruch Ha'Shem.*"

I can feel myself bracing for the moment when the man

standing before me dramatically pulls off his Rabbi Bob mask to reveal the new, curmudgeonly replacement rabbi. But he doesn't. Instead, he just smiles as he scratches his big, round belly. "As fate would have it," he says, stroking his beard, "we had to move on to Plan B."

"Plan B?" I ask.

"You're stuck with me for a little while longer. I can explain more later," he says, "but for now, have a seat, Avery. We were just in the middle of discussing the Jewish tradition of *bikkur cholim*, or visiting the sick." He looks at all of us and asks, "Has anyone here performed this *mitzvah*? It's a big one."

Little Basha's hand darts up. "My pet rabbit had a cold last winter and every day I brought her carrots and more carrots and more carrots and then she got better and then she died."

Rabbi Bob is quiet for a few seconds while the rest of us sit there looking confused and slightly bothered at the same time. Finally, he says, "How wonderful that your pet rabbit was loved and cared for so deeply up until the end. May her memory be a blessing."

Little Basha's hand is still raised when she adds, "Beardy. Her name was Beardy. Because it looked like she had a beard on her face. And her memory *is* a blessing because she always made me laugh. Except for the time she bit me and I cried."

"Thank you, Basha. Well, as I was saying, *bikkur cholim*—or visiting the sick—is a very important *mitzvah* in the Jewish tradition. It's part of the greater tradition of *gemilut chasadim*—the giving of loving-kindness. As you have probably noticed," Rabbi Bob continues, "our friend Gideon is not with us today."

Little Basha, whose hand is *still* up in the air, calls out, "Is he dead?"

Rabbi Bob smiles and says, "No, no, not at all. Far from it! He's home this week due to a football injury, from which he will undoubtedly fully recover. A little extra rest is all he needs." Rabbi Bob leans over and whispers to Basha, "Why don't you put your hand down now? I'll take more questions and comments later." Little Basha nods and folds her hands in her lap while her legs keep swinging under the bench.

"In keeping with the tradition of caring for the sick, I thought it would be wonderful for all of us to put together a get-well basket for Gideon, and I'll arrange to have it delivered this week. Even though he's not up for many visitors right now, this could be a way for all of us to show him that we care and wish him a speedy recovery."

Little Basha's arm shoots straight into the air as she calls out, "Carrots! I'll add the carrots to the basket!"

"Yes, that would be fantastic! Who doesn't love carrots?" Rabbi Bob chuckles. "Today, in your smaller Maccabi groups, you'll be making cards for Gideon and coming up with a list of items, carrots included, to put in his get-well basket. So, without further ado …" Rabbi Bob shoos us away with his hands, "… onward with your loving-kindness!"

Going Rogue (at Hebrew School)

Thank you God thank you God thank you God ... Those are the words running through my head the whole way to Morah Neetza's class. Which is weird for two reasons: 1. I don't even believe in God, and 2. I've never felt grateful for anything in Hebrew school.

When I get to the classroom, Morah Neetza has the big table set with a stack of colored paper, markers, glue, glitter, and stickers. "Make somesing beautiful," she tells us, "like zis." She holds up a huge card with a glittery blue flag of Israel and Gideon's name spelled out in falafel ball stickers. "I very much like to make cards," she admits.

I decide to make a Star Wars themed card. I'm deep in my rendering of Luke's training session with Yoda in the swamp when Rabbi Bob comes up behind me. "Yes, Jedi strength flow from The Force!" he says in that familiar Yoda voice. I never thought I would have been happy to hear it, but I am.

"Is this seat taken?" he asks, pointing to the empty chair beside me.

I shake my head.

His knees creak as he lowers himself into the chair. "Surprised I'm still here?" he asks in his regular voice.

"Kind of," I admit.

Rabbi Bob smiles. "So am I."

"So why are you? I mean, why are you here?"

"Never one to shy away from questions, are you?" He switches back to Yoda's voice and adds, "An excellent Jew this makes."

Rabbi Bob takes a deep breath through his nose. I'm wondering how grown-ups can make nose-breathing sound so loud when he says, "The new rabbi had a delay in her arrival. She's moving from another country, actually. Ran into some red tape getting her visa squared away. But it'll get straightened out, I'm sure."

"So you're here until then?"

Rabbi Bob nods. "Okay with you?"

"I guess."

"And if memory serves correctly, I owe you some lightsaber training."

I think his memory isn't serving him correctly. "But I broke your lightsaber. Remember?"

"And I fixed it. After all, I'm the one who built it. I should know how to fix it, don't you think?"

"*You* built it? How is that even possible? Where did you get the kyber crystal? How did you get the blade to emit like that? What makes the hum so real? Have you ever killed someone with it? And why is it so heavy?"

Rabbi Bob laughs and says, "No, Avery, I have not killed anyone with it. Sorry if that's a disappointment to you. As for the rest of your questions—I may be a rabbi, but I also happen to be a man of science, like yourself. Before I became a Force-sensitive rabbi, I studied mechanical engineering."

A scientist rabbi? There is a small explosion in my head. And apparently, it has vaporized words, because I am speechless.

"Not what you expected, is it?"

I slowly shake my head.

"You didn't think it was possible, did you? That a person of science and a person of religion could be the same person?"

"But it isn't possible." The words trickle from my mouth.

"On the surface, perhaps. But it's the contradictions between religion and science that I believe have made me both a better scientist, and a better Jew."

"How?"

"It's a matter of shifting our gaze from answers to questions." Rabbi Bob leans forward and rests his elbows on his knees so that we're eye to eye. "People are hungry for answers. Some think they will find them in religion. Others believe they will find them in science. And, to some extent, both are right. But, from my experience, at least, the two are not mutually exclusive."

"I don't know what 'mutually exclusive' means."

"It means the universe is much too vast, and complex, and beautiful for only one thing to be true—for only one way to observe and appreciate the world around us. One of the best parts of being a human is that we don't have to choose sides." Rabbi Bob nods to his lunch bag, sitting on the table, and adds, "Another best part of being human is the invention of the pastrami sandwich on rye. A little brown mustard and a dill pickle on the side. Throw in some potato salad and call it a day." He closes his eyes and kisses his fingers.

I'm pretty sure all this talk about food has made him forget his point. But I'm wrong, because after he finishes daydreaming about his sandwich, he opens his eyes and says, "The real beauty of Judaism is the value it places on the question. For thousands of years, Jews have been seeking, asking, wrestling, learning, and—I like to hope—growing, adapting, even flourishing. Likewise, for the scientists, seekers who revel in the richness of life's mysteries. The moment we believe we've got all the answers—whether in science or religion—is the moment we begin to fear the unknown. And that fear, my young Padawan, is the surest way to The Dark Side."

"But you just said we don't have to choose sides. Isn't that the whole point of Star Wars? That there's good guys and there's bad guys and everyone chooses a side?"

"I would like to answer your question with a question," Rabbi Bob says. "Has anything ever turned out to be *not* what you expected?"

"*Yeledim!*" Morah Neetza calls out, "Time for snack. Bring me your cards." She puts out a big bowl of grapes on the table. "Wash your 'ands and we will say our *beracha* for the food before we eat. No blessing, no food!"

I look at my unfinished card for Gideon.

"Gideon," I say to Rabbi Bob. "He's not what I expected."

But the truth is, a lot of things aren't turning out as I expected. Being on the Bears. Damon. Rabbi Bob is looking at me in a way that makes me sure he's pulling a

Jedi mind trick because the next thing he says is exactly what I'm thinking.

"Hebrew school isn't what you expected, is it?" The words hang in the air for a little while. Then Rabbi Bob says, "You have football practice today after Hebrew school, is that correct?"

I nod.

"I have an idea. What if I do a little shopping for Gideon's basket after school while you're at practice, and then you can come with me to bring it to Gideon. I think he'll be very happy to see you. We can check in with your mom to make sure she's okay with that plan."

•

Without Gideon and Damon, practice was extremely uneventful, although a lot of the players were still a little hyped up from Sunday's win. Final score: fourteen to seven.

First win of the season and I missed the end.

Weirdly, I don't feel that upset about it. Guess I can just add this to the list of things that didn't turn out as I expected.

Rabbi Bob shows up at the end of practice driving an old blue minivan.

"Am I late?" he asks as I climb into the back seat of his car. I've never been in the rabbi's car before. In fact, I've never been in *any* rabbi's car. Not to mention I never really considered the possibility of rabbis driving cars at all. Don't rabbis just live in synagogues? That's how I used to picture them, anyway, like trolls under a bridge. I'd be lying if I said I didn't have a slight nuts-in-chocolate-chip-cookies feeling in my gut, like I'm not exactly sure I belong. But I squeeze in anyway, pressed against a giant basket filled with stuff in the back seat of Rabbi Bob's minivan.

"I think I went a little overboard," Rabbi Bob says, tilting his head toward the overflowing basket. A package of cookies spills out. As I pick it up to stuff it back inside, I read the label: *Ma's Famous Chocolate-Chip Macadamia Nut Cookies*. Nuts in chocolate-chip cookies. They actually look pretty tasty. I wonder if this is the universe trying to send me a message.

CHAPTER
25

Tuesday, Later

"*Erev tov!*" Yapa says with a wide grin as he opens the door. "Do I have that right? *Erev tov?* It's been a heck of a long time since I set foot in that synagogue of yours. My Hebrew's gotten a little rusty over the years, just like the rest of me!" Not surprisingly, Yapa has an unlit soggy cigar dangling from the corner of his mouth. Is it the same one every time? He's wearing a black French beret tilted to the side and a t-shirt covered in fake burn holes that says WHO FARTED?! on it.

"Yes, perfect, Mr. Munk. *Erev tov* and good evening to you, as well," Rabbi Bob replies. "Love your house, by the way. A real stand-out. A place where the imagination has been set free."

"And why shouldn't it?" Yapa booms as he ushers us in. "Please, take a walk on the wild side." I've got the basket in my arms, but it's piled so high with food, magazines, books, games, and the cards we all made that I can barely see the top row of masks hanging on the wall. There's even a Star Wars Lego set squished in the middle of the basket. "All that stuff for me?" he jokes. "You really shouldn't have!" Yapa pulls a carrot out of the side of the basket and chomps into it.

"It's for Gideon, actually," I reply.

"Even better!" Yapa says, taking another huge bite out of the carrot. "The kid will be thrilled to see you. He's been bored as a docked sailor. Doc says we need to limit his stimulation. Most exciting thing he's done since Sunday is brush his teeth."

"Why don't you bring him the basket, Avery?" Rabbi Bob says. "I'll sit back with Mr. Munk to catch up. It's been a while, hasn't it?" He pats Yapa on the shoulder and smiles.

"How about I brew a fresh pot of coffee? You hungry? Just pulled out a batch of my famous chipotle brownies from the oven!"

"Sounds great!"

"Gideon is in his room, Avery. Top of the stairs, turn left."

I carefully balance the basket in my arms as I make my way up the creaky wooden stairs. I find Gideon sitting cross-legged in the middle of his bed, which is under a canopy of little silvery stars dangling from invisible threads. He is wearing an ewok suit. The room is dark except for the light coming from a lava lamp in the corner. His hands are resting on his knees and his eyes are closed. I set the basket down on his desk. His eyes blink open.

"Did you ever notice how the back of your eyelids are like a movie screen?" he says calmly. "If you look at it long enough, pictures start to light up and move. I was just watching the constellations reconfigure themselves into what I believe was an underwater Gungan ice-cream party on the planet of Naboo. Jar-Jar Binks was scooping up flavors I never saw before."

"Wish I could come."

"You can, if you stare at the back of your eyelids long enough."

Other than opening his eyes and talking, Gideon hasn't moved an inch. The lump on the side of his head is still there, but smaller and less red. "Does your head hurt?"

"Not really. The headache is mostly gone."

"We brought you this basket of stuff," I say. "Everyone at the synagogue, I mean. Rabbi Bob says it's part of a tradition. He brought me here. He's downstairs talking to Yapa."

Gideon pulls out a bag of gummy worms from the basket. "I like this tradition." He opens the bag. "Want one?"

We sit there in silence chewing on gummy worms. We get about halfway through the bag when Gideon says, "I wonder if anyone is bringing a basket to Damon."

"He doesn't go to our Hebrew school."

"I guess," Gideon says unconvinced.

I shrug and bite the head off of a gummy worm.

He adds, "But Damon's still hurt, right?"

"All right, Gideon, I've got to ask: What is up with you and Damon? I cannot figure it out. And, honestly, it's bugging me. I feel like I'm watching Luke hand an ice-cream cone to Darth Vader every time you act nice to that guy. And in case you didn't notice, Luke *never* gives ice cream to Darth Vader. He's not supposed to. What he's supposed to do is slice off his hand in a deathly lightsaber battle. Not that I expect you to slice off Damon's hand in a deathly lightsaber battle. Although … I have to admit, the idea isn't half bad."

"Nah. Not my style," Gideon says.

"Okay, so it's not your style. But I still don't get it. Why are you so nice to him?"

Gideon thinks quietly for a moment, then slowly looks up at me. "Because I get the feeling no one else is."

The words hit me in a strange way. Even though I heard them through my ears, I feel them sinking into my chest like something warm oozing through the cracks in a suit of armor.

•

"That was such a good time, don't you think, Avery? What a lovely family," Rabbi Bob says in the car on the way home. "That Yapa—a real character!"

Somewhere in the back of my mind I register the words that Rabbi Bob is saying, even though I'm not really paying attention. "Yep," I say. Probably a trick I learned in Hebrew school, just in case I get called on. Like a way of hearing but not really listening. The thing is, my mind is distracted. Still feeling Gideon's words oozing.

"Did you have a nice time with Gideon? I'm sure he loved seeing you."

"Yep." What was Gideon's point, anyway? Of course no one is nice to Damon. Why should anyone be nice to Damon? He's not nice to anyone!

"Yapa says he's doing well. Should be back at school next week."

"Yep." Is his point that Damon would be nicer if people were nicer to him? Because if that's his point, it's a dumb point.

"Did you try those chipotle brownies? Wow! Got quite a kick to them. Yapa sent me home with a whole plate of them. Here, go ahead and have one." Without taking his eyes off the road, Rabbi Bob hands back a plate piled high with brownies and wrapped in plastic wrap.

"Yep." I hold up my hand to pass on the brownies. If Damon and Elmo from *Sesame Street* were the last two living creatures on earth, I bet Damon would still call Elmo *dill weed*. And no one is nicer than Elmo. Scientific fact. So if Gideon feels bad for Damon because no one is nice to him, he's got it backwards.

"Did Gideon love all the goodies in his basket? I imagine the Lego Star Wars set was a hit. Not to mention the gummy worms."

"Yep." It *would* be pretty nightmarish to have everyone

hate you, though, wouldn't it? I mean, even if you deserved it. Now that I think about it, it's true, what Gideon said, about no one being nice to Damon. His dad is always shouting, and everyone is too afraid of him to actually like him. He doesn't really smile, either. I've never seen him laugh. He cackles. And even though a cackle kind of looks like a laugh, it's basically the polar opposite.

"Hey, Avery, do you love Hebrew school more than football and Star Wars combined?"

"Yep." Damon *was* kind of nice to us at the hospital, wasn't he? I mean, not *nice*, but not mean. Definitely not mean. It was normal nice. And that little wave was totally un-Sith-like.

"Ha! Gotcha!" Rabbi Bob cries. I snap to attention. Our eyes meet in his rearview mirror. "You haven't really listened to a word I said, have you?"

"I guess not, sorry."

"What's on your mind?"

"Nothing."

"Nothing? Doesn't seem like nothing."

"It's just something Gideon said." I pause. Headlights pass by in the night. The turning signal in Rabbi Bob's car sounds loud in the silence. The warm oozy feeling in my chest isn't going away.

"Rabbi Bob?"

"Yes, Avery."

"Do you have to be Jewish to get a basket? For that thing you talked about. The visiting the sick thing."

"*Bikkur cholim?* No, of course not, Avery. The giving of loving-kindness has no boundaries." Our eyes meet again in the rearview mirror. "Why do you ask?"

"No reason."

Rabbi Bob chuckles. "Shall I use my Jedi mind tricks to extract information?"

"It's just that … you're going to think this is weird … but, you know … another kid was hurt pretty bad during that game. Not just Gideon."

"Yes, I was there, remember? He was the evil Sith you brought to the ER."

I nod.

"How is he?"

I shrug.

"Ah, I see," Rabbi Bob strokes his beard as we wait at a red light.

"His name is Damon," I mumble.

"And you're thinking you might like to bring something to Damon, since he's injured."

I shrug.

"But it feels totally counter-intuitive because you don't like Damon. In fact, you don't like him so much that you chose to battle him in my office. Or, at least, the idea of him."

I nod. Rabbi Bob wasn't joking about using Jedi mind tricks to extract information.

The light turns green, but instead of going straight, Rabbi Bob pulls over. "Do you suppose evil Siths like chipotle brownies?" he asks with a wink.

Despite everything I have learned thus far about good guys and bad guys, I find myself nodding. Luckily, though, I still have the sense to hold back my smile.

CHAPTER
26

Tuesday Evening

After a phone call home to check in with my parents about our plan, and to get Damon's address from the EBFL roster, Rabbi Bob and I are on our way.

The whole drive there I'm actually thinking this is a terrible idea. But some other part of me is telling me I should still do it. I don't know why. And, for better or worse, that part is louder.

By the way, if this whole idea is a bust and Damon ends up murdering me on his front doorstep then, for the record, I blame Gideon and Rabbi Bob in equal parts.

•

We pull up to a very orderly-looking brick house. The grass is perfectly mowed and the shrubs are perfectly trimmed. Even though all the leaves are coming down from the trees this time of year, I can't find one single dead leaf anywhere on their property. An American flag is flapping on a pole in the corner of their yard.

Please don't be home please don't be home please don't be home, I chant under my breath the entire walk from the car to the front door, kicking myself for having this stupid idea. The phrase *temporary insanity* comes to mind. Rabbi Bob knocks on the door using the huge eagle-shaped metal knocker. No one answers. Unfortunately, he knocks again.

"Well, looks like no one is home," I state the obvious. "Guess we could just leave the brownies by the front door and—"

Footsteps. Someone is coming. I pretend like I don't hear it. "—get going?"

Darth Damon's dad's wide, leathery face appears through the window on the side of the door. The Imperial March begins to play.

The door opens. "Can I help you?" His voice is very deep.

"Hello, sir. My name is Rabbi Bob and this is Avery." I feel like an idiot standing there holding a plate of brownies. Like I might as well be in a bunny suit holding a basket of Easter eggs.

"I know who he is," Damon's dad snaps, pointing at me. He stares at us, not saying a word. At this point, I would prefer to be just about any other place in the galaxy. And this includes the lava-filled planet of Mustafar.

"We understand that Damon is laid up for a little while,

and we wanted to bring something to cheer him up," Rabbi Bob explains. "It's a gift on behalf of his teammates, Avery and Gideon, as well as the rest of our little Jewish community at Temple Sinai. Perhaps you're familiar with the synagogue, right up there on Maple Street?"

I feel dizzy listening to Rabbi Bob say so many words.

"Right, I know it," Damon's dad says. "My father used to do the building maintenance there, before he passed away."

"You're kidding!" Rabbi Bob says, smiling. "What a small world, isn't it? Please, tell me your father's name."

"Ed."

"Well, thank you to Ed, may his memory be a blessing, for the care and maintenance of our beloved little old synagogue." A goofy smile freezes across Rabbi Bob's face.

No one knows what to say next and it feels like a thousand years before, finally, Damon's dad grumbles, "If you're looking for Damon, he's on the couch watching *Dead Meat.*"

Rabbi Bob suddenly looks worried. "It's a TV show," I whisper. He looks relieved.

"DAMON!" his dad booms. "YOU HAVE COMPANY!" The plate of brownies rattles in my hands. Why did I think this was a good idea?

"Please, let him be. We'll find him," Rabbi Bob says.

"Suit yourself." Damon's dad points, "He's that way."

I follow Rabbi Bob into a dark room with a couch. A bloody shoot-out scene is blasting on the TV. As soon as

Damon sees us, he sits up and turns it off. He looks at us but doesn't say anything.

On an awkwardness scale of one to ten, the level in the room is currently hovering around twelve. I can feel Damon's dad behind us, looming.

"Hello, Damon. I'm Rabbi Bob. And you know Avery."

"What's up," he mumbles.

"Hey," I quietly say. "These are for you."

"It's a little something, to help with your recovery," Rabbi Bob adds.

"Cool," Damon says.

I set down the plate.

"Damon, what do you say?" his dad barks from behind me. I jump a little.

"Thanks," he says.

A thousand more awkward moments of silence pass before Rabbi Bob says, "So, how are you feeling today, Damon?"

"All right."

"Good, good," Rabbi Bob says.

I unfold and refold my arms across my middle. I study the gray carpet.

"I understand your grandfather worked at our little synagogue," Rabbi Bob says.

The awkwardness level rises to fifteen.

Damon shrugs.

We did the good deed, I'm thinking, *can we go now? Please?*

"Well, we wish you a speedy recovery, Damon. And we

hope you enjoy the brownies. They're chipotle. Might want to wash them down with a glass of milk."

"I like spicy," Damon says.

"Then you'll love these! Gideon's grandfather made them. It was Avery's idea to bring some over," Rabbi Bob explains unnecessarily.

"Okay, then," I say as I start to back out. "See you around. Feel better."

"Second to that," Rabbi Bob says, "feel better soon, Damon. It was a pleasure to meet you." We start to leave.

"Gideon okay?" Damon calls out behind us.

Rabbi Bob smiles. I answer, "Yeah, he's okay."

"Cool," Damon mumbles.

CHAPTER

27

The Following Spring

"I just don't see how it's possible," I tell the rabbi. "If the bush burns, how is it not consumed? I mean scientifically, how is that even possible? Like, did fire work differently back when Moses was shepherding his flock in Egypt? Was it a special kind of biblical fire that covers a bush, doesn't burn it down, and talks like God?"

"Oh, no, Avery. The bush wasn't talking *like* God, the bush was talking *as* God," Rabbi Estévez tells me, as if this detail will clear everything up. Then she turns to Rabbi Bob, who is sandwiched between Gideon and Little Basha on the bench, and says, "*Claro que si, Roberto*. I see what you mean about this one. Restless with questions." And then she turns to me and says, "Can you imagine how boring learning would be without questions?"

"Dreadful!" Rabbi Bob cries out.

"*¡Que pesadilla!*" Rabbi Estévez chimes in Spanish.

Sometimes she says things in Spanish, probably because she's from Panama. "A real nightmare!"

"Borderline *dangerous!*" Rabbi Bob adds.

They look at each other and laugh and laugh. I'm glad they're having such a good time at my expense. Meanwhile, neither rabbi has answered my question. And the longer they laugh, the more I am sure they never will.

Rabbi Estévez steps down from the *bimah*, where she had been reading to us about the story of Passover. She looks much shorter at ground level. In fact, Rabbi Estévez might be the shortest grown-up I've ever known. When she first started in January, the synagogue had to have a new podium specially made for her because she could barely see over the top of the old one.

"I'm four feet, nine and three-quarters inches tall," she announced proudly from a step stool behind the old podium. It was Little Basha who asked. "At my height, the three-quarters inch is significant, even if it's coming from my frizzy gray curls!" She patted her frizzy gray curls.

And now, as she steps closer, Rabbi Estévez looks at me with her big brown eyes and says, "Listen, Avery, there are many ways to understand a rainbow." Her purple flowing sleeves flap as she demonstrates the arc of a rainbow in the sky. "We can talk about the dispersion of light from moisture in the air and why it takes the form of a multi-colored arc. We can analyze how master artists like Rubens or Chagall painted them on canvas. We can read Norse, Greek, and Aboriginal mythology to discover how they made meaning of the rainbow. We can simply go outside in search of one."

Little Basha's hand shoots up but she doesn't wait to be called on. "We can get a box of Lucky Charms cereal! There are rainbow marshmallows in there! I ate them myself!"

Rabbi Bob chuckles and pats Little Basha on the back. He leans over and whispers, "My personal favorite way to understand a rainbow."

"Which one is right?" Rabbi Estévez asks.

"The scientist's explanation," I argue, "the one about the dispersion of light. Because that's *really* what a rainbow is."

"When I look at a rainbow, I don't see the dispersion of light." Gideon's slow, raspy voice crackles. "I hear music. Drums, mostly. Sometimes a tuba."

I turn to Gideon. "A tuba? Really?"

He nods. "I thought everyone did."

That's my best friend for you. Hearing tubas at the sight of a rainbow. "Man, Gideon, they better preserve your brain for scientific research after you die. Who knows what discoveries lie in that blobby mass of gray and white matter?"

"May he live until a hundred and twenty!" Rabbi Estévez and Rabbi Bob cry out in unison. Sometimes I wonder if those two were separated at birth. Maybe it's just because they went to rabbi school together a million years ago. That's how Rabbi Bob got her to be our new rabbi. She was moving back to the area to be closer to her grandchildren. He asked if she wanted a rabbi gig.

"Think of the story of Passover like a rainbow," Rabbi Estévez tells us. But this doesn't answer my question. I can't let it go.

"Rabbi, if I think of the Passover story like a rainbow," I reason, "then wouldn't there be at least one scientific explanation for how the bush burned but was not consumed?"

She squints her eyes at me, like she's trying to focus on a hunch. She pokes me in the chest with her stubby finger. "I don't know why I like you, Avery, but I do!" Then she raises her eyebrows and says to Rabbi Bob, "Call me *loca*, *Roberto*, but I think we may have a rabbi in the making over here."

Rabbi Bob's eyebrows dance up and down as he smiles. "Agreed."

I shake my head in disbelief. "*Me*? A *rabbi*? I think I have more of a chance of becoming an armadillo than a rabbi."

"But armadillos don't ask such important questions," Rabbi Bob says. "And you, Avery, do. Always thinking, always asking, always looking to shine light through the cracks. This is what would make you an excellent rabbi."

I never thought of myself that way, but the idea of being a light-shiner is pretty cool. "Like some kind of a mystical spelunker," I say.

"Exactly. Like a mystical spelunker," Rabbi Bob replies with a smile. "Of course, you would also make an excellent Jedi Master," Rabbi Bob says. He checks his watch. "Rabbi Estévez, if it's all right with you, I believe these young

Padawans are due for their weekly training." A shower of "Yes!" rains down.

Even though Rabbi Bob supposedly retired, he still comes every Sunday for an hour of Lightsaber Torah. Lightsaber Torah is basically a lightsaber tournament, but with a Jewish theme. Gideon and I invented it at the end of last fall after Rabbi Bob *finally* gave us our lightsaber training. The training was supposed to be just for me—I only had to wait forever for it—but how could I keep such a thing secret from Gideon? He's not a violent person, but I'm pretty sure he would have killed me if I'd left him out. So, after our training, Gideon said something like, *I think Hebrew school would be better with lightsabers.* And I said, *Only like a million times better.* And Rabbi Bob said, *Why not?*

Then we started planning how it could work. Gideon and I focused on the maneuvers—I through VII—and how to teach them, and how to structure the weekly tournaments. Rabbi Bob made a bunch of simple lightsabers—small ones for the Maccabi Haifa kids, bigger ones for the Maccabi Tel Aviv kids—and a bunch of special tournament t-shirts. They're black with white letters that say *Yud is for Yoda.* *Yud* is a Hebrew letter I've heard burped by Gideon many, many times. Cracks me up every time.

When Rabbi Estévez came along, she agreed to work with Rabbi Bob on the things we were supposed to learn from the Torah. So after we study the text with Rabbi Estévez, Rabbi Bob guides us through lightsaber combat, where we battle out our ideas and questions about the text using our lightsabers. That way we really have to know our stuff. Gideon and I go around and help the younglings perfect their form. We both agree that Little Basha is the most Force-sensitive.

"Padawans, lightsabers on!" Rabbi Bob commands, and the light of ten glowing lightsabers hums to life.

"Wait! Wait for me!" Morah Neetza comes jingling in. "Don't start wizout me!" She tosses off her neon-pink jean jacket, picks up the spare lightsaber, and joins the group. She taps her butt. "I'm telling you—ze lightsaber training is better for ze *tukkhes* zan my Zumba class!"

I give the instructions. "Jedi ready position, focusing on III, dominant foot back, blade in vertical position." They all follow my command. "I love saying stuff like that," I whisper to Gideon as I walk past him.

"I know," he whispers back, not turning his gaze for a second from his current opponent, Little Basha. I'd say the odds are sixty-forty that she wins this round.

I cue Rabbi Bob.

"Padawans, Round One begins with this," he bellows dramatically. Everyone holds still in ready position. "In the Book of Exodus, God inflicts ten plagues upon the Egyptians as punishment to Pharaoh for not letting the enslaved Jews leave with Moses. *What are the ten plagues?* Bonus points for naming them in the order in which they were inflicted!"

Lightsabers begin to dance as kids call out various plagues. "Turning water into blood!" "Frogs!" "Lice!" "Wild animals!" "Diseased livestock!" "Boils!" "Thunderstorm of hail and fire!" "Locusts!" "Darkness!" "Death of firstborn!"

I walk around, making sure that everyone's form is correct and that, under no circumstances, is anyone aiming for Zone 1. Zone 1 is the head and, apparently, the first place most people want to strike. I learned this the hard way after our first tournament, when Little Basha tried to slice off my head at the neck.

Rabbi Bob tosses me a lightsaber. "Shall we?" he invites.

I start listing the plagues in order with each strike of my lightsaber. Rabbi Bob forms an impressive Circle of Shelter to block my penetration. By the time I get to *a thunderstorm of hail and fire*, I have to ask. "A thunderstorm of hail *and* fire? Really? You want to explain how that's even possible? I mean, even if it were, wouldn't the hail extinguish the fire, or the fire extinguish the hail?"

Rabbi Bob laughs as he ducks under my Hawk-Bat swoop. "And," I continued, "am I supposed to believe that frogs just fell from the sky? Was it across all of Egypt, or just around Pharaoh's village? And don't even get me started on *rivers of blood* or *death of firstborn*. Come on … *death of firstborn!* Grown-ups worry about too much violence on TV? If you ask me, I'd say they should worry about too much violence in the Bible!"

By now, Rabbi Bob is panting and sweat is dripping into his beard. Guess I got carried away striking during my little rant. "Break!" he calls. Everyone sets down their lightsabers. "Get some water, back in two minutes!" he huffs. Rabbi Bob takes a long swig from his big coffee mug that says, *Come to The Dark Side ... We Have Cookies.* By the time everyone is back, he looks more ready than ever for the next round.

"Round Two is in honor of the mystical spelunker, Avery Hirshel Green," Rabbi Bob announces, and I'm thinking maybe I should have kept my mouth shut.

"Every year, Jews recite the ten plagues as part of the Passover Seder," he begins. "In doing so, are we inappropriately celebrating the suffering of the Egyptian people? How do you think the Egyptians felt when they were being punished by God? Can you hear the cries of the Egyptian mothers and fathers at the death of their firstborn?" Kids are silently paired up in ready position looking like they're actually focusing on Rabbi Bob's questions, even the Maccabi Haifas. "Do you believe in a God who punishes people?" he asks. "What was the cost of our freedom?"

I slowly walk around the room. Morah Neetza is hopping back and forth from foot to foot. "You're not in a Zumba class," I quietly remind her. She settles into a more Jedi-like stance.

Rabbi Bob strokes his beard. "Should the freedom of enslaved people be obtained at any cost? Discuss among yourselves ... and begin!"

I watch as everyone battles out the questions, the room filling with discussion and the deep, musical hum of lightsabers in action. From the corner, Rabbi Bob catches my eye. He broadly sweeps his hand, as if he's presenting everything happening in the room to me. As if he's answering my question.

"WOO HOO!" Gideon cries out as he leaps into the air, making a fast slash against his opponent.

"Oh, no you don't, Mister!" Little Basha hollers. She swings her lightsaber high above her head. "Not so little anymore!" she growls, then takes a perfect Form IV swipe at Gideon's knees.

Rabbi Bob and I exchange knowing glances, as if this week's Champion of Lightsaber Torah just presented herself. I stand there for a minute, taking it all in.

The thing is, even though it's gotten way more fun, I still don't always get the point of Hebrew school. And I still have a million more questions. But I guess that's okay—or maybe better than okay. Maybe that's how it is when you're searching for places to shine a light. I pick up my lightsaber and turn to Rabbi Bob, smiling. "Ready for the next round?" I ask, armed with my lightsaber, and something even more powerful—my questions.

NOTES

p. 15: *Well, thank you for volunteering to stay after school for as long as it takes to learn the entire Torah while standing on one foot.*

There is a famous story about two great Jewish scholars, Shammai and Hillel, who lived in ancient Babylon more than two thousand years ago. One day, a man interested in converting to Judaism approached the scholars and suggested that he would convert to Judaism if they could teach him the whole Torah while standing on one foot.

Shammai, who was very strict in his approach to the Torah, was greatly offended by the stranger's suggestion that the Torah could be learned so quickly. He threw the man out of his tent.

Hillel, on the other hand, was a very humble and patient man. He said this: "What is hateful to you, do not do to your neighbor. That's the whole Torah; all the rest is commentary. Now go and study it!"

When Avery is terrified that Rabbi Bob will keep him after school to learn the entire Torah while standing on one foot, he forgot Hillel's story!

p. 32: *"Shalom, Avraham," he bellows across the room. "Welcome to the goodliness of our tent!"*

When Rabbi Bob says, "Welcome to the goodliness of our tent!" he is referring to the prayer called *Ma Tovu*, which everyone is singing when Avery enters the synagogue. *Ma Tovu* is a special prayer that Jews often recite upon entering the sanctuary where services are held.

Ma Tovu can be translated as "O How Good" or "How Goodly". The first line of the prayer was said by a man named Balaam, who was not Jewish. In fact, he was sent by King Balak of Moab to put a curse on the Jews! But when he approached the Jews in their place of worship to deliver the curse, he was so struck by the beauty of the place and everyone worshiping inside that instead of cursing them, he said: *How goodly are your tents, O Jacob, your dwelling places, O Israel!*

This is the only prayer used in Jewish services that was not written by a Jew. The rest of the prayer is:

As for me, through Your abundant grace, I enter your house to worship with awe in Your sacred place.
O Lord, I love the House where you dwell, and the place where your glory tabernacles.
I shall prostrate myself and bow; I shall kneel before the Lord my Maker.
To You, Eternal One, goes my prayer: may this be a time of your favor. In Your abundant love, O God, answer me with the Truth of Your salvation.

p. 33: *I shuffle up to the front row and try not to puke. I have never been this close to the* bimah *in my life.*

The *bimah* is a raised platform at the front of every synagogue where the Torah is read, and where the rabbi leads services. Anyone called to read from the Torah will stand on the *bimah*. Avery is not too happy about being put near the *bimah* in front of the class!

p. 103: *Rabbi Bob chuckles. "If I didn't know any better, I'd think you were Moses at the burning bush." He gives me a little nudge toward the lightsaber. "Go ahead, you can touch it."*

The story of Moses at the burning bush comes from the Book of Exodus, the second of five books of the Torah. In this story, we learn about the life of Moses, who was born to a Jewish mother, Jocheved, but had to have his Jewish identity kept secret in order to survive in a land hostile toward Jews. Because of the brave and clever acts performed by his mother and his sister, Miriam, Moses was able to be raised safely as a secret Jew by the Pharaoh's daughter in Egypt. As a young man, Moses leaves the palace and discovers the miserable lives of the enslaved Jews. During this time, Moses witnesses an Egyptian beating a Jew. His pain and anger over the incident cause him to kill the Egyptian. After this, Moses must flee to Midian where he becomes a shepherd. Meanwhile, life for enslaved Jews becomes even worse at the hands of the Egyptians. One day, while tending to his flock, Moses sees a most strange sight—a bush that is burning but is not burned up. He goes to the bush to investigate. The voice of God speaks to Moses through the burning bush, reminding him of the suffering of his people. God explains that he has chosen Moses to carry out the task of rescuing his fellow Jews. At first, Moses is terrified and rejects God's request. He explains that he is not capable of carrying out such a heroic task. But God assures Moses that He will stay with him and perform miracles to force Pharaoh to let the enslaved Jews leave Egypt.

When Avery first saw the lightsaber, he looked as shocked as Moses did at the sight of the bush that burned but was not consumed. It's possible Avery was even more shocked than Moses, but there are no sources to confirm this.

p. 181: *With two fingers, Rabbi Bob checks his pulse at his neck. "I'm afraid I'm still very much alive. Baruch Ha'Shem."*

Baruch Ha'Shem is a common expression used among more observant Jews to mean "Thank God." *Ha'Shem* means "the Name" in Hebrew, and the literal translation of the Hebrew expression *Baruch Ha'Shem* is "Blessed be the Name." Why this expression? Because many observant Jewish people follow the practice of restricting the use of God's name outside of a strictly religious context.

p. 207: *"May he live until a hundred and twenty!" Rabbi Estévez and Rabbi Bob cry out in unison.*

The expression, "May he/she live until a hundred and twenty" is a common Jewish blessing. In Deuteronomy, the fifth book of the Torah, Moses' age upon his death is given as one hundred and twenty. More importantly, Moses is described as being in great mental and physical condition when he dies at this ripe old age. So the blessing, that one should live until one hundred and twenty, is a blessing for a long and healthy life.

ACKNOWLEDGMENTS

I wrote *Going Rogue (at Hebrew School)* because I didn't think I could answer the question one more time. The question, of course, was: Why do I have to go to Hebrew school? My three kids asked me every week, sometimes many times a week. I gave short answers, I gave long answers, I gave thoughtful answers, I gave quick answers. I answered every which way I could imagine, and just when I thought I'd given them the perfect answer—the one to prevent them from ever needing to ask me again—what would happen? Right! One, two, or even all three of them would ask me again! Eventually, I got the idea to write a book about it, secretly hoping that a book would settle the question once and for all.

But having an idea is very different from making the idea come true. There's no way I could have turned the idea of a book into an actual book without help from a lot of people.

For my sons, Erez, Soli and Gabriel: thank you for being an endless source of inspiration. Thank you for being honest critics and for all of your suggestions. Each one of you thinks this book is about you ... and each one of you is right! It's also about all the kids who, like you, have wondered why their parents make them do the things they do, or who ask the kind of tough questions that no one seems able to answer. Keep wondering and searching. Answers do come, just not always in the form you expect or as fast as you hope.

Thank you to Catriella Freedman, Madelyn Travis, and all of the generous, dedicated folks at PJ Our Way and the Harold Grinspoon Foundation. Without your support, turning my idea into something kids can hold would be much less possible.

Thank you to Michael Leventhal for taking a leap of faith into the world of children's book publishing, and for bringing me along. Thank you to Jessica Cuthbert-Smith and Steve Williamson for putting it all in the right shape.

Thank you to SCBWI. For anyone with the idea to write or illustrate books for young readers, joining SCBWI is your start.

To the Temple Achavat Achim community in Gloucester, Massachusetts—*todah raba!* A special shout out to Rabbi Steven Lewis for being at the helm of the ship, and to Cantor Bruce, for singing funny songs, telling funny stories, and using funny instruments. My kids may not admit it, but I have caught them smiling in Hebrew school more than once because of you. "I Didn't Learn a Thing in Hebrew School" is one of our faves.

To Phoebe Potts, thank you for helping parents like me link the past to the future, and for doing it with heart, wisdom, elbow grease, and humor.

Thank you to Rabbi David Cohen-Henriquez, for advising me in the way of The Force.

Thank you to Mom, Gail, and Dad for loving me and cheering me on.

Thank you to everyone who read various drafts of this book, including Ursula de Young, Lori Baker, Eve Loftus, Joan Brunetta, Sarah, Jacob and Abram Kielsmeier-Jones, Laila Goodman and Casey Andrews. To Leslie Brunetta, thank you for telling me that I am a writer. Thank you to Peter Loftus, Chief Scientist. To my critique group: Sharon Abra Hanen, Chelsea Dill, Shannon Falkson, Alison Goldberg, Beth Jones, Kate Narita, Jennifer Barnes, Hayley Barrett, and Rajani LaRocca—thank you for being my writing home base.

And for my husband, Eliran, who believes in me every day. Thank you for giving me the time to do this, and for bringing the kids to Hebrew school week in and week out. I did my best to explain why.